John J. Fox

Blood

John J. Fox

Blood

ISBN/EAN: 9783337389703

Printed in Europe, USA, Canada, Australia, Japan

Cover: Foto ©Andreas Hilbeck / pixelio.de

More available books at **www.hansebooks.com**

An Original Comedy,

IN FOUR ACTS.

By JOHN J. FOX, M. D.

BOSTON:
PRINTED BY J. W. PITMAN & SON,
No. 23 WATER STREET.
1879.

DRAMATIC CHARACTERS.

Marquis Max Muddle.	Countess de Foy.
Gabriel Hamilton.	Mrs. Breeze.
Mr. Breeze.	Laura Bliss.
Earl de Foy.	Lady Carra.
Colonel Lyon.	Madam Buzot.
Dr. Craft.	Mabel Buzot.
Lord Carra.	Lady Max Muddle.

Sporting Characters, Gendarme, Old Women, and Servants.

BLOOD.

ACT I.

SCENE I. — *A Street in Paris. Enter two sporting characters.*

First Sport. Talk about kissing, do you suppose a French kiss has the real smack in it?

Sec. Sport. Suppose you inquire under the first female nose you meet.

First Sport. Just what I will do, and I'll wager you a night's sport that I get it.

Sec. Sport. I'm your man on such a bet.

First Sport. Now, then, for my woman and the kiss. [*Both look, one up, the other down the street.*] By all the dressmakers in Paris, here she comes. [*Enter ragpicker with basket on her arm.*]

Sec. Sport. Come, Jack, you'll find it under her nose somewhere.

First Sport. By all the gods in a heap, old woman, if rags were at a premium, you would be a prize.

Old Woman. And if fools were worth as much as rags, I would fill my basket.

Sec. Sport. Look, Jack, 'twill hardly be fair unless you discriminate between lips and wrinkles. [*Exit old woman.*]

First Sport. [*Looks after her, while the other laughs.*]

Sec. Sport. That kiss will spoil before you get it.

First Sport. Not if you will renew the bet.

Sec. Sport. Certainly, I can safely do it, for you are too modest to bet and win on cheek.

First Sport. [*Looks up and down the street.*] Just let some Virginia step this way and we'll see.

Sec. Sport. The first one's grandmother, for instance.

First Sport. Draw back, there she comes, and for a granny, if such she is, she takes very good care of her wrinkles ; look [*Enter Countess de Foy, with her face closely veiled*] here my beauty.

Countess de F. Please, sir, don't detain me ; I'm in a hurry, and my time is short.

First Sport. Well, now, my pretty rosebud, what's the price for a peep at thy face?

Countess de F. [*Looks anxiously in direction from which she came, then turns indignantly around.*] A gentleman to look at it. [*She tries to pass him, whereupon he catches her and tries to kiss her. She struggles to get away, and drops a bracelet. Enter Earl de Foy. Sporting characters fly. The Countess falls as if in a faint. The Earl stoops and attempts to look in her face. Enter Gabriel Hamilton, who pulls the Earl over on his back and assists the Countess to her feet.*]

Gab. H. Lady, go your way. I will see that neither this rough, nor his associates, molest you again.

Countess de F. [*In a disguised voice.*] Thank you, sir, thank you. [*Exit Countess.*]

Earl de F. Look here, sir, there must be some mistake ; I supposed that lady was my wife.

Gab. H. Wife! So you thought you would get a crowd of roughs to knock her down, that you might see. [*Enter Gendarme.*] Here, sir, arrest this man for attempting to rob that lady. [*Pointing after the Countess.*]

Gendarme. Then, sir [*addressing the Earl*], you come with me.

Earl de F. Hands off, sir, I am a nobleman.

Gendarme. Indeed, who'd think it ? [*Exit Gendarme with the Earl, his prisoner, followed by Gabriel H.*]

SCENE II. — *Ante-room in the house of Madame Buzot.*

Countess de F. I was to meet the Earl here early this evening. Have you seen anything of him yet?

Mme. Buzot. We have not.

Countess de F. I hope you won't, while you wish me to enjoy myself.

Mme. Buzot. I shall be pleased to see you enjoy yourself all night.

Countess de F. Thanks, I'm sure you're very kind.

Mabel B. Well, gentlemen and ladies, what say you to a game of " *ecarté,*" while we wait for the company's arrival.

Gab. H. I am willing to be somebody's poor partner.

Countess de F. Then I'll have pity on you and take you for mine.

Mabel B. So it appears, Marquis, there is nothing left for us to do, but to take pity on each other.

Marquis Max M. Yes, and we can beat them at that game, as well as this.

Mme. Buzot. By the way, Mr. Hamilton, we expect a countryman of yours here to-night, with his wife and grand-daughter. It seems they bring the young lady out for the first time.

Mabel B. I'm sure she is old enough to show herself, and ought to be able, at her age, to feel at home in the drawing-room, as well as in the nursery.

Countess de F. Probably her parents have had the best of reasons for keeping her secluded.

Mabel B. And, without doubt, only allow her appearance to-night on condition that she puts on her best behavior.

Gab. H. Ladies, this is hardly fair, as you say she is my countrywoman, and, as yet, you have never even seen her. Now, perhaps, you will find her to be a well-behaved and well-informed young lady.

Countess de F. Oh! we presume she has something of a knowledge of etiquette, a pianoforte ability to the extent of " The Maiden's Prayer," and probably with the aid of an artist, who would daub out her endeavors and leave his own, she might be able to paint a landscape, with a cow in the foreground and some sheep in the distance.

Mabel B. Yes, and perhaps before leaving home, she, with the aid of a servant, worked a monkey in worsted for her sweetheart, in order that he might forever be reminded of her when he saw it.

Gab. H. If this before you know her, what afterwards?

Mabel B. Ah, but we do know something of her already. For instance, she is very wealthy,—wealthy enough to buy a lord, earl, or marquis, and has just come to market to look up one.

Gab. H. My defence ceases. If there is another of that wit at large you cannot speak too severely of her. To hear of such characters from one's country is enough to make every honest American blush.

Mabel B. Her grandmother told mother herself that she had the blood of a noble exile in her veins, and so was determined to wed her grandchild to a title.

Countess de F. And she will.

Gab. H. Why so positive ?

Countess de F. Because we've always a large stock of bankrupt noblemen on hand, ever ready to go with the highest bidder.

Gab. H. Indeed, it's a pitiable sight to see some old object of flesh, flash, and vanity, running over the continent, with a sixteen-year-older at her heels, hair crimped and puffed, and lost in her own estimation and dry-goods refineries, — ready to love a lord at first sight, or sigh in the ear of some moustached Adonis of this so-called noble blood. Born in a land of freedom, yet ever ready to cringe and do homage to any fop, dandy, or booby, who has a handle to his name. [*The Marquis deals.*]

Mabel B. Partner, you never give me a good hand. [*The Marquis holds his hand out to her.*]

Marquis M. M. Is not that a good hand ?

Mabel B. Yes, 'tis very *hand*some.

Countess de F. The trump hand of roguery.

Gab. H. That is, you mean a *tricky* hand.

Countess de F. Yes, good at all kind of games.

Mabel B. We ought to beat them, Marquis. They seem to think you have a good hand. I wish I could think as much. I am sure that you must have been dreaming of this American young lady when you made this deal. How is it, have you been considering how you could let her capture you to the best advantage ?

Marquis M. M. No, I was just thinking how fast she could run a mile, or rather how much champagne she could drink before she would get——let me see, I must have been thinking of something else, if I had a thought at all; yes, I was wondering whether she was like that other American woman, Miss Toadstool,—I always get that name mixed up with frogs and things,—yes, that's it, Miss Froginham.

Mabel B. Oh! you mean Miss Frothingham, she who has been so long on the market.

Countess de F. Yes, poor thing, she is rather unfortunate in making a market. However, she boasts of having had the offer lately, from that English nobleman, Lord Crescent, but which she said she declined on account of a few discrepancies in his organism.

Mabel B. Well, now, I supposed she had got too desperate to have any choice in the matter.

Countess de F. I wonder if she took into consideration the fact, that, if he has a glass eye, the other is good if it is crossed, and as for his club-foot, I am sure that's an impediment for any wife to be proud of in a husband, that is provided she don't wish him forever running after her.

Mabel B. Why yes, and he could make all the lady that's possible to make of her, just as well as if he didn't have a glass optic and club-foot.

Gab. H. And she boasts of this as a conquest?

Countess de F. Yes; but my lord vows if ever he made her an offer, 'twas when he was intoxicated.

Gab. H. Oh, well I presume she'll find some one yet, who'll succumb to the personal charms of her money.

Countess de F. Who's severe on your countrywoman now? Why the poor thing's horse ran away with her the other day, and she narrowly escaped being killed.

Gab. H. I should judge by your estimation of her, that nothing but a horse, mule, or ass would run away with her.

Mabel B. Well, now, she does at times seem modest.

Marquis M. M. Yes, modest enough to approach a bottle or take a man's knee for a stool.

Countess de F. Good gracious, Marquis, has she been proposing to you, too?

Marquis M. M. Oh no, I didn't encourage her.

Mabel B. Why, Marquis, what does she lack to make you a wife? Isn't she rich?

Marquis M. M. To be sure. That's her great virtue.

Countess de F. Isn't she a woman ?

Marquis M. M. Undoubtedly, or she never would have taken such a fancy to me.

Countess de F. Isn't a willingness to be married a failing of hers ?

Marquis M. M. Well, I judge she wouldn't have any serious objections to be so taken in.

Countess de F. And pray, isn't she old enough ?

Marquis M. M. She must be, if any stock 's to be taken in wrinkles.

Countess de F. And now, to be candid, wouldn't she be, to say the least, good-looking, if it were not for her mouth ?

Marquis M. M. My idea exactly. If she didn't have a mouth she'd be a success, or if she only had it under her back hair, or somewhere where it couldn't be seen, why then I think she might at least put in an appearance. [*Ladies and gentlemen pass and repass the door, laughing and talking in dumb show. Mabel rises and the rest follow her example.*]

Mabel B. I see the company is beginning to arrive. [*They move about the room and all finally exit but Gabriel and the Countess.*]

Gab. H. My lady, I think I have found the owner of this bracelet.

Countess de F. [*Takes and examines it.*] True enough, where did you find it ?

Gab. H. Where some roughs assaulted a lady this evening.

Countess de F. I am under a life-long obligation to you, and believe me, I shall not forget it. But the Earl ?

Gab. H. I called a gendarme, who arrested him for an attempt to rob an unknown lady.

Countess de F. Thanks, 'twas a favor I will remember.

Gab. H. Madam, you altogether overrate so slight a service. I took you, as of course you were, a stranger to me, till I was introduced to you this evening, and your name recalled at once the name upon the bracelet.

Countess de F.   I presume since, you have been wondering what brought me into the street alone with my husband after me at that time of the night.

Gab. H.   Of course it surprised me.

Countess de F.   Dear me! [*Sighs.*] The Earl's not old enough to be my father, the one great misfortune of my marriage, but the worst of it is he's jealous of me. You don't know how often I wish he was engaged in some kind of business, or had a commission in the army or navy,—in fact, anything to do but to nurse his spleen. That's the worst of having a man of leisure for a husband.   Then he thinks my eyes were made but to dwell on him, just as if he were handsome and single.   Now I let him support me as a husband should, and even allow it to be generally known that we are married, but he is not satisfied with that,—in fact, he is the most ungrateful specimen of a married man I ever saw.   There, there, there's no end to the poor recommendation I could give him.

Gab. H.   [*Smiling.*] Indeed, madam, you are to be pitied.

Countess de F.   Indeed, I am.   I'd rather be in mourning for him than lead this kind of life any longer.

Gab. H.   So you thought you'd don a suit to-day to see how it would become you.

Countess de F.   Of course, I always keep a suit on hand, in case such a sad event should occur.

Gab. H.   Why, is there any probability of his dropping off, without giving sufficient notice?

Countess de F.   'Twould be just like him, especially if he thought it would annoy me to have to delay his funeral for a day, just to have a suit made.

Gab. H.   Then you're all ready to mourn for him?

Countess de F.   Yes, and anxiously waiting.

Gab. H.   And have you made all arrangements for his final exit?

Countess de F.   I have performed my part, and am all ready for him to do his.

Gab. H.   With a wife's fortitude?

Countess de F.   Certainly, as a wife is expected to mourn at short notice, in case there is a mournful rending

of ties and snapping of heartstrings. I feel it my duty
to be all prepared to perform a bereaved wife's part,—
and even with willingness resign myself to fate and
widowhood.

Gab. H. And perhaps you have selected his grave ?

Countess de F. Not quite, though I have my eye on
a good-sized lot,—room for a dozen or more, you know.

Gab. H. And inviting enough to make a husband's
retreat ?

Countess de F. And very convenient to make a wife's
last resort. And now, my dear sir, if you're done quiz-
zing me, I'll tell you how I came in the street alone this
evening with my husband following me. Well, toward
evening, I concluded it would be a good time for me to
make a certain charity call, and so donned myself in
black, wishing to make the most out of my walk, and
absorb, if possible, a little comfort out of the reflection
that I might at least be taken by somebody for a widow.

Gab. H. Then you fancy a widow's weeds ?

Countess de F. Certainly, for if anything in my estimation becomes a woman, it is to be in mourning for her
husband. [*Looks at him coquettishly.*] Well, I started
out, and on my way accidentally met a friend, who very
kindly accompanied me to my destination, and then part
way home again, when, though dark, I insisted upon
going the rest of the way alone, and so we parted, just
as I observed a man, who proved to be the Earl, approach-
ing us,—after which he seemed to follow me up to the
time you witnessed the assault.

Gab. H. Then did he really follow you ?

Countess de F. I thought so at the time, but now
think he was only hurrying home from the club, as he
frequently comes that way.

Gab. H. It's surprising that you did not make yourself known, and thus prevent his arrest.

Countess de F. Not for the world would I have him
know it was I. You see, he saw me part with my friend,
and also would have found me in black, and out after
dark, three circumstances that would easily make a man
like him, given to jealousy, suspicious. So for the peace
of what mind he has, I concluded that 'twould be better
for him to know nothing about it, and, of course, as a

gentleman and a friend, I can depend on you to keep my
secret.

Gab. II. Most assuredly madam, 'twill be as you
wish.

Countess de F. Thanks, I will remember the obligation, but come, let's to the drawing-room. There, no
doubt, you will find an array of young ladies who have
palpitating abilities, ogling eyes, and who for a sigh
would be happy to thus entertain you. [*Exit Gabriel
with Countess on his arm.*]

SCENE III. — *Drawing-room,* — *with company assembled.*

Marquis M. M. America, I presume, is a great country to raise Americans in, — that is, I should say, — a
country of vast importance to itself.

Mrs. Breeze. Yes, Marquis, America is a very large
country, with vast resources.

Marquis M. M. Large as France ?

Mrs. B. Quite.

Marquis M. M. France is a mighty nation ; nothing
like it in this country. It is, to speak figuratively, a
nation of French people.

Mrs. B. Very true, much unlike the English.

Marquis M. M. Yes, yes, I can safely say I never
saw an Englishman who was not a Johnny Bull.

Mrs. B. I see, Marquis, you have made a deep study
of national characteristics.

Marquis M. M. 'Twould be affectation to deny it, for
if we were all of a mind who'd be the wisest.

Mrs. B. I must say, Marquis, that you're very eccen-
trically profound.

Marquis M. M. Thanks, Madam, I am happy to find
you, like most of your countrywomen, given to appreciation rather than flattery.

Mrs. B. Yes, Marquis, I think if you ever visit
America, you will find appreciation a national char-
acteristic.

Marquis M. M. I have often thought I would like to
visit your country, and even live there if I couldn't do
any better, but I dread being sea-sick, and not seeing as
many sea-serpents as other folks.

Mrs. B. I doubt your being sea-sick, Marquis, and my impression is that only persons of *delirium tremens* temperament ever behold sea-serpents.

Marquis M. M. Well, it may require a peculiar gift to see those snakes, but to invest in the *delirium tremens* only requires an overdose of intoxication.

Mrs. B. [*Aside.*] Perhaps he's the president of some temperance society ; so I'll just draw him out. [*Aloud.*] Accidents will happen, but then we can all avoid intemperance.

Marquis M. M. True, Madam, I have known a man to die after smoking a cigar. [*They go up the stage, and Gabriel and Laura come down.*]

Laura. Indeed, we've noble company here to-night.

Gabriel. Yes, could titles make them such, we have ; but as it is, we've some noble, because high nature tried her best, and did a noble act in making them, and in whom she laughs to scorn the puny efforts of a vain, mutually titled, aristocratic royalty, whose work at making noble flesh, blood, and human passions, seems but a fool's parody on Heaven's highest art.

Laura. Then you think these titles but the humor of folly?

Gab. H. I think they add neither physically, mentally, nor morally to the individuals who bear them, and are nothing more than vain epithets.

Laura. At least they have the value of a name.

Gab. H. True, if we did not call my lord,—my lord,
  why then,
To designate him we'd call him something else ;
Now if that something else was plain, blunt Mr. Smith,
How nature o'er his soul, her reign would then assert.
Now, his title seems a charm against her sway,
And the inspiration of his affectation.

Laura. I see the romance of royalty has no charms for you.

Gab. H. To read of royalty and its long train of noble kin and titled followers,
With characters ennobled by the pen
And lofty feelings of some bard or scribe,
'Tis fine.

Then royalty seems from the gracious hand of God :
Each king, a sceptre tempered with justice,
Each queen, a diadem of purity and love,
Each prince, a signet from the hand of Jove,
Each princess, the crown's purest jewelled gem,
Each earl, a diamond from blemish free,
Each duke, a ruby with a lustre great, ,
Each lord, lady, and knight, pearls from out the ocean of
　　humanity,
And all a glittering chain, right royal enough
To hang upon a nation's neck.

But take them as they are, do we here see our ideal counterparts in these realities, whose power and title seem but licenses to their ignorance, arrogance, and passion ! [*Gab. and Laura go up the stage, while the Marquis and Mrs. Breeze, followed by Mr. Breeze, come down.*]

Marquis M. M. I presume, Madam, your family was somewhat related to Europe in the past ?

Mrs. B. Oh, yes, our family is a very old one. I couldn't for the life of me say where it commenced.

Mr. B. [*Aside.*] That's about the only thing she don't know about her family.

Mrs. B. My great grandfather was cousin to the Duke of Twopennyshire, England, but was beheaded for being engaged in a conspiracy against his lawful king and country. He was also a near relative to the celebrated Baron Strutter, who fell in a duel with Gen. Prodder.

Mr. B. [*Aside.*] She don't say anything about that other relative of hers, who, while trying out soap fat, fell into the vat and was tried out himself.

Mrs. B. You see such men are to be revered for their noble lives and heroic deaths.

Marquis M. M. Yes, we should think of such men only to forget them.

Mrs. B. I see, Marquis, you can be witty.

Marquis M. M. Well, you know, one can't help laughing for amusement once in a while. Yes, Mrs. Breeze, I fought a duel myself, once.

Mrs. B. Indeed ! an affair of honor, I presume ?

Marquis M. M. Honor, oh no, nobody's honor was

questioned. It was a mere point of veracity between me and a woman.

Mrs. B. A woman! I thought as much.

Marquis M. M. You see, at court one night, the Princess Maria stepped on my foot, and didn't even as much as ask my corn. Then, just to be a little entertaining, I ventured on the insinuation that she had a foot of her own, and could, for one who never made a parade of her feet, crush a fellow's little toe with great delicacy; and may I never kill my man again if I did not receive a trayful of challenges the next morning. Of course I accepted everything, and we met and all acknowledged the corn, and made her feet as small as apologies would admit, but the baron who then championed the cause of her feet, and since married her, has often wished that I had killed him then.

Mrs. B. Then they don't live happily together.

Marquis M. M. Well, I presume he knows how much of a foot she has by this time.

Mrs. B. She is a princess of blood, I presume?

Marquis M. M. Oh yes, that's the only kind we have in this country.

Mr. B. [*Aside.*] There it is again. Ever since I've been worth a barrel of pork, with her it's been nothing but blood; blood, blood. [*Aloud.*] But the case is different with me, Marquis, for I can't swear that I ever had a father or mother. As for grandfather or grandmother, I'm positive on that point. And for great grandparents, I was never accused of having any, so you see we make Mrs. Breeze's old fossils do for the whole family. [*Mrs. B. tries to catch Mr. B's. eye.*]

Marquis M. M. Never had any parents?

Mr. B. Not that I know of; you see it's decidedly vulgar to have parents. Why sir, even mules have parents and make no great kick about it either, and, indeed, in our country, it's a common thing for fools to have great grandparents, and I've taken particular notice that they never seem much the wiser for it.

Marquis M. M. Well, Mr. B., I hope you like France?

Mr. B. Oh yes, we've found France to be all that we expected, but were sadly mistaken about England. You see, all the people there belong to the royal family, and so we came to France for good company. Why, sir, begging is allowed there even in the House of Lords. Positive fact, every time the Queen marries off one of her children, she has to beg the price of the honeymoon from the people. Paupers, we call them in our country, where there is a good deal of respect paid to the dictionary. I presume the reason they don't enforce the law there against begging, is, that they'd have to put the Queen in the poor-house if they did.

Mrs. B. Marquis, can you tell me who that gentleman is with my granddaughter?

Marquis M. M. Let me see, I think he came, stop [*as if in a study*], from the country Columbus discovered.

Mrs. B. The West India Islands?

Marquis M. M. I think it's part of those islands.

Mr. B. Perhaps you refer to America.

Marquis M. M. That's it; he's an unknown cipher from America.

Mrs. B. Only an American! why, bless me, I thought he was a lord.

Mr. B. How stupid!

Mrs. B. I'd never have known the difference if I hadn't been told.

Mr. B. To be sure.

Mrs. B. How blind I must have been.

Mr. B. Now be careful and don't get caught napping again. You must know that this is an unpardonable mistake, and, I presume if Mr. Hamilton knew, he would never forgive you. [*Gabriel leaves Laura and joins the Countess.*]

Mrs. B. Excuse me, I must go to her at once, as he has left her.

Marquis M. M. Madam, don't you think if I and your daughter were introduced, we would soon get acquainted?

Mrs. B. Certainly, Marquis, I should be pleased to see you friends. [*They join Laura just as Lady Max Muddle and Lady Carra come up the opposite side.*]

Lady M. M. Indeed, he couldn't be more out of place if he were an hostler.

Lady Carra. Certainly not; and I'd just like to know whether his presence among us is an intentional insult or not.

Lady M. M. And see, even the Countess ogles him as though he were a prince. I wonder if she knows his real character. [*The Countess and Gabriel separate in dumb show; Countess approaches the group laughing.*]

Countess de Foy. Indeed, I can give Mr. Hamilton the credit of being the best flirt I ever knew.

Lady M. M. [*Seriously.*] My dear Countess, are you aware that this Hamilton is a mere nobody, and out of his place here?

Countess de F. Then, my dear, suppose you find it for him.

Lady M. M. I was just saying he'd make a splendid valet for the Marquis.

Countess de F. Don't you suppose you could pick out one of these ladies, who'd also make a good governess for him? [*Turns away.*]

Lady M. M. Ha, ha, an intrigue in the bud!

Lady C. Her poor taste has become chronic, and will be sure to kill her yet. [*Lady M. M. and Lady C. go up the stage, followed by the Marquis.*]

Mrs. B. And this, then, is the person from whom you've been accepting attentions all the evening!

Laura B. He seems a gentleman, if he is poor.

Mrs. B. Yes, a poor gentleman.

Laura. Who to-night has acted a more perfect gentleman than he?

Mrs. B. That but speaks well of his acting, and I shouldn't wonder if he were some doubtful character in disguise.

Laura. A prince IN COG., for instance.

Mrs. B. Prince of knaves, no doubt; but what possesses you to feel called upon to defend this stranger so, when even our hostess, who is supposed to know him, offers but a lame excuse for his presence among us? [*Gabriel approaches unseen.*] A poor American indeed, — see that you cut him at once and compromise yourself no further. This wise proceeding will leave him no further passport to your presence, and I shall see that he don't intrude. [*They go up the stage without observing Gabriel.*]

Gab. H.   So this is she who has come to Europe to invest in one of fashion's strutting-jacks,—she, an angel for a dream,—an ideal for love's fancy,—a heart's love at first sight; and she, with sense and wit, a heart, no doubt, and yet has come to sacrifice herself on folly's altar! No, no, I'll not believe it; I'm sure I'd wrong her if I did. [*Countess approaches Gabriel.*]

Countess de F.   Why, Mr. H., you look as solemn as some married man, who has just heard of his mother-in-law's recovery from a dangerous illness.

Gab. H.   I was just thinking——

Countess de F.   [*Laughing.*]   No doubt,—men will think, and women will be the topic,—but cheer up, for 'tis evident that Lady Max Muddle is badly smitten with you, for she thinks you'd make a splendid valet for the Marquis.

Gab. H.   Not insulting at all.

Countess de F.   Oh, no, that would be unladylike, but as it is, she's only a little free-hearted with her abuse. You see, since she found out that the "*Breezes*" are rich, the young lady an heiress, and Mrs. Breeze delighted with the Marquis, she goes into perfect ecstasies over everything American.

Gab. H.   Especially over me.

Countess de F.   Oh, I presume she counts on you to Americanize the Marquis, in order that he can court the young lady in the manner most familiar to her. I declare, if here isn't the Earl. [*Goes to meet him.*]

Gab. H.   [*To himself.*]   By Jove, this report of my poverty has worked wonders in the faces of those around me; but SHE—will it make a change in her? Will it sour her smile and freeze her face when I am by? No, no, I'll not believe it, and yet, suppose I put it to the test. I will.   [*He crosses to Mme. B. and they talk in dumb show.*]

Marquis M. M.   [*Aside.*]   Yes, I'll have her. I wouldn't like a more solemn performance than to manufacture her into a lady; with me 'twould be a mere sleight-of-hand.   Ah, they're forming for the dance, and I think-

I might just as well invest my arm around her waist for
a short time. Let me see, what will I say? Permit me,
Miss, to tread toes with you; no, though that's a literal
rendering of the truth, I presume I'm not to know that
she has toes. [*Aloud to Laura.*] Miss, I beg pardon,
your name stifled my mind, but shall I have the pleasure
of dancing with you?

Laura B. You must excuse me, sir; I have concluded
not to dance.

Marquis M. M. [*Aside.*] Refused, and for nobody!
Thunder and lightning! I wish there wasn't any danger
in fighting a duel; blood would fly; I'd assert my honor
as a gentleman and a nobleman.

Mad. B. [*To Mabel.*] It seems, Mabel, that there's
a report among the company that our friend, Mr. Hamilton, is nobody but a poor American student.

Mabel B. You, of course, gave this story a most em-
phatic denial?

Mad. B. The strangest part of it is that Mr. Hamilton told me the story himself, and even requests us not to
deny it.

Mabel B. Not to deny it! Strange, I should say!

Mad. B. But who could possibly have started such
a story?

Mabel B. The Countess, of course.

Mad. B. Why think you it was she?

Mabel B. Because it has the characteristics of her
falsehoods, and besides, she quizzed me about him, and
not getting any satisfaction, she, of course, told this
story in order to draw us out in his defence.

Mad. B. But this is strange of him.

Mabel B. I presume he thinks he can start a little
romance with poverty for a basis, but I think he'll find
that women generally know with whom they romance.
Of course, it's all very well to fall in love with a poor
young man, if one only makes sure that he'll turn out
rich on the wedding-day.

Mad. B. That, of course, is the lady's look-out.

Mabel B. But did he give his motive for allowing
this story to go undenied?

Mad. B.   Whimsical sport, or something to that effect, he said.

Mabel B.   It makes it awkward for us.

. *Mad. B.*   Well, I presume we must humor him so long as 'tis at his own expense.   In fact, my dear, 'twill make your chance all the better to have it so, for while others will cut him with contempt, we can treat him like a prince.   [*The company prepare for the dance.*]

Marquis M. M.   [*Aside.*]   By Jove, cut, and left on the floor to dance with my anger!   Ah, there's Lady Carra all alone, so I'll just take a shuffle with her, if she is well anchored.   [*He approaches and asks her to dance in dumb show.   The dancing commences.   After waltzing awhile the Marquis and his partner come to the front of the stage, where she has a fainting fit and falls into his arms.   He struggles to let her down easily, and partly succeeds, when he slips and goes down plump with her on top of him.   The dancers crowd around: he holds her head up, and while attempting to wipe her face with his hand-kerchief, gets the paint off her cheeks and dye off her front hair, all over her face in streaks.   Then he lays her down in desperation, and off comes her back hair; she chokes, he slaps her on the back, and out come her false teeth.*]

Gab. H.   What's the matter?   Has the lady fainted?

Mr. B.   Not if I know anything about fits.

Mrs. B.   My dear, don't you know the difference between a spasm and a fit?

Mr. B.   Forbear the distinction.

Mrs. B.   Poor dear, she looks delicate.

Mr. B.   Yes, I shouldn't wonder if she'd be dead in fifty years from now.

Countess de F.   Her hair came out quickly for such a short sickness.

Mrs. B.   True enough, just see her hair.

Mr. B.   Yes, her poor ringlets are scattered round like pigtails on the floor of a slaughter-house.

Mad. B.   Well, Marquis, how did this happen?

Marquis M. M.   Don't know; the first thing I knew, I felt as if I was wrestling with a nightmare.   When she tumbled, she didn't take me into consideration at all, but went off in a variety of directions at once.

Mrs. B. The poor dear danced well.

Mr. B. Yes, but I should have thought she'd stayed at home when it's her day to have a fit.

Mrs. B. Fit!

Mr. B. Yes, and now tell me I don't talk fit.

Marquis M. M. Well, Mr. Breeze, then you call this a natural kind of a fit.

Mr. B. Yes, very natural and decidedly original.

　　　　　　　　　　　　[*Enter Lord Carra.*]

Lord Carra. Sir, what is the meaning of this?

Marquis M. M. The natural freak of a fit.

Lord C. But how came her face in that condition?

Marquis M. M. A peculiarity of her blushing, I presume.

Lord C. Her friends say you wiped her face with the same handkerchief you used on your boots.

Marquis M. M. I deny it. [*Takes out the handkerchief and shakes it.*] There it is. I deny your friends' gusto, and take this privilege to tell the truth.

Lord C. Sir, we shall meet again. [*He helps Lady Carra to her feet.*]

Lady C. [*Faintly.*] My dear, you forget yourself.

Lord C. True, but I'll not forget him. [*They start to go.*]

Marquis M. M. But look, my Lord, you forget your wife's teeth.

Lady C. Yes, my teeth, my teeth. [*She faints again.*]

Marquis M. M. [*Aside.*] A duel! By Jove, this is hot. [*Takes out his handkerchief and wipes his face, covering it with streaks of black and red. The company laugh and curtain falls.*]

ACT II.

SCENE I. — *Drawing-room with door in the centre leading to veranda; windows on each side of the door, through which are seen lawn, croquet-players, with ladies and gentlemen on veranda watching the game.* [*Enter Laura.*]

Laura. I presume the poor fellow is wondering by this time who sent him the money. Well, as nobody knows it was I, who can say I acted unladylike? Being an American, he ought to be able to hold his head up with the rest of them. Besides, merit like his should not be allowed to suffer, while any woman's pin-money can do so much for it. I only hope it reached him in time, and enabled him to reject such a menial position as valet to the Marquis. [*Exit Laura. Enter Mad. and Mabel Buzot.*]

Mad. B. So it seems that all our advice to Mr. Hamilton has gone for naught.

Mabel B. Just think of it, valet to the Marquis.

Mad. B. Oh, there's no accounting for what these Americans will do when inspired with the notion.

Mabel. B. Don't you believe he has some other motive than mere sport, for accepting such a position?

Mad. B. I don't see what it can be. [*They go out on the veranda. Enter Laura with a letter in her hand. Enter Marquis from veranda.*]

Marquis M. M. I should think Miss Bliss that you'd be afraid when you're here all alone.

Laura. Not at all: why, on such occasions as this, I really enjoy it.

Marquis M. M. Aren't you afraid?

Laura. Of what?

Marquis M. M. Of ghosts, and men, and things.

Laura. Oh, no; I don't believe in ghosts, nor men, nor things.

Marquis M. M. Why, I've seen the biggest ghost I ever saw.

Laura. Indeed!

Marquis M. M. Yes, besides that, I know the true romance of a reliable ghost story.

Laura. A ghost story! Do tell it, will you, while I read this letter.

Marquis M. M. Well, she was a maiden.

Laura. Who, the ghost?

Marquis M. M. Yes, she was a maiden or a woman, I can't say which; however, she was a female, of that I am sure.

Well, a young man fell in love with her, but she, it seems, did not return his negotiations, more on account, I presume, of there being plenty of other fellows in the world, than she did from having any particular dislike of his sex, for she like most women would rather be deluded than otherwise.

Then, it seems, he looked in another direction, for he began to multiply the bad habits of his youth, and develop his family traits of dissipation, with all modern improvements, such as parting his hair in the middle, and making pets of his bottles. For variation he counted the stars, and made a hobby of the man in the moon, and showed a preference for other things of less consequence. Then he commenced to resist his beefsteak and onions; sleep with his eyes open; and waste his wind on sighs and love-ditties. Of course this kind of courting, like every other kind of a good thing, had an end, and so he was finally winded, and died of hydrocephalus of the heart; caused, some said, by drinking too much.

Then he turned ghost, and appeared to his lady-love in his night-clothes, and she was petrified with astonishment and collapsed into a faint, and before she came to, was introduced into eternity. Then, disguised as ghosts, they appeared to their parents, scared them to death, and like a bubble they eloped from mortal vision. [*After a pause.*]

Laura. Oh, what did you say?

Marquis M. M. Why, that the lovers made use of the next world by getting into it; that is, they were inveigled beyond the reach of mortal nose pryers.

Laura. Then they died.

Marquis M. M. Yes, they were spirited away. [*He attempts to sit down to the piano, but slips from the stool and partially falls, both arms striking on the key-board with a crash. Enter Lady M. M., Mad. B., Mrs. B., Mabel and Countess de Foy.*]

Lady M. M. Good gracious, Marquis, what's the matter?

Marquis M. M. Oh, nothing, I—I—I only slipped and fell against the piano. I thought you might like a little music.

Countess de F. So you gave us an overture.

Lady M. M. Then you're not hurt.

Marquis M. M. Oh no, I'm used to falling you know.

Lady M. M. Used to falling! What do you mean?

Countess de F. Oh, he only means that he has his ups and downs like the rest of us.

Marquis M. M. That's it, especially the downs.

Lady M. M. [*Takes up a splendidly bound album and glances through it.*] Ah, Mrs. Breeze, I see you've quite a collection of our friends' photographs.

Mrs. B. Yes, and some day I expect to prize them above value.

Lady M. M. [*To the Countess.*] There, isn't that good for the Baron Bodkin.

Countess de F. Very good, indeed; his deformities take as natural as life.

Lady M. M. But what in the world possessed him, with such a nose and chin, to have a profile taken.

Countess de F. Possibly because he's ashamed of the other side of his face, though I never gave him credit for such good taste.

Lady M. M. And true enough, if here isn't his poor wife, looking as natural as her shadow.

Countess de F. Mustn't she feel flattered though, when she looks on him as her lord and master.

Lady M. M. I wonder what ever induced them to have each other.

Countess de F. Probably 'twas a mutual agreement to take each other in; he took her possibly in an insane moment, and with her, no doubt, 'twas any port in a storm.

Lady M. M. How self-possessed-looking our Lady Annie Fuss is, though.

Countess de F. Yes, she possesses herself, and it seems no one cares to compete with her for the prize.

Lady M. M. But it appears she still has faith in paint.

Countess de F. And undoubtedly, too, in rehearsing the marriage ceremony to herself. But I'm afaid that's as far as the poor thing will ever get, though she is still willing to fall in love with a man if he only looks cross-eyed at her.

Lady M. M. Of what a sinful waste of sighs she must be guilty.

Mrs. B. It's too bad the poor dear is so afflicted with the headache.

Countess de F. Well, I for one don't object to her aches at all, but this forever looking around for a soft place to put her head, when we all know it's soft enough to put anywhere, makes it a conspicuous matter of affectation, not to pass unnoticed.

Lady M. M. I vow, if here is n't the Princess Maria.

Countess de F. [*Looks.*] True enough, and wrinkles will take.

Mabel B. Mother, we were talking about her age the other day, and concluded that the Marquis knew something about it.

Lady M. M. Why, bless you, child, she was marriageable when the Marquis was a boy.

Marquis M. M. Yes, and had a moustache.
[*Altogether in chorus.*] A moustache!

Marquis M. M. Yes, on her lip.

Countess de F. And I'll warrant 'twas not the first moustache she had there either.

Marquis M. M. It may have been a chronic mole.

Countess de F. Or down, that had reached its maturity.

Lady M. M. Well, I can say with truth, 'twas more than the Marquis had, when he was only as old as she pretends to be now.

Mabel. Don't you think she paints?

Countess de F. Oh! no; but she's troubled badly

with a chronic blush, caused no doubt by her husband's
ignorance. Poor thing, she's always in awful trouble
when he's around. She married, as she supposed, a
man of a negative character; but bless your soul, if
you saw them together, you'd sigh for the mistake she
made.

Laura. [*Aside.*] And these are the kind of people
whose photographs grandma expects to prize above value.

Lady M. M. Bless me, whose apparition is this?

Countess de F. Why, that's Lord Wild's better half.
I should think you'd know her by that assumed air of
innocence, of which she makes a specialty.

Lady M. M. There, I knew there was something
familiar-looking about her, but thought it was the heav-
enly inclination of her nose. And if her isn't our
Lady Annie out in another endeavor.

Countess de F. And as usual, for her trouble and
money, of course, got sympathy and poor photographs.

Lady M. M. How manly she looks.

Countess de F. Yes, but that's more than can be
said of her husband. [*The Marquis' head falls on his
shoulder and he commences to snore.*]

Lady M. M. For the Lord's sake, Marquis, what's
the matter?

Countess de F. Just let me give him a sniff of my
salts; he's faint. [*Lady M. M. shakes him while the
Countess puts her vinaigrette to his nostrils. He springs
out of his chair.*]

Lady M. M. [*With a serious look.*] Why, my dear,
what is the matter?

Marquis M. M. Struck by lightning in the nose.

Lady M. M. [*Aside.*] Oh! the ass, to go to sleep
here, and snore too, with the Breezes present. [*Aloud.*]
My dear, you are not well.

Marquis M. M. Especially my nose.

Lady M. M. I thought there was something wrong,
you've been looking so weary to-day.

Marquis M. M. Yes, I've been trying to think of
something till I got all tired out.

Countess de F. Was it about that English lady who
tried to induce her coachman to elope with her?

Marquis M. M. No, it was about an hymeneal scrape.

Countess de F. It's too bad you can't remember it, such troubles are always so spicy, refreshing, and entertaining.

Mabel. Perhaps 'twas about Lady Familiar, who, while attempting in a sane moment to cut her husband's throat, sliced his nose off.

Lady M. M. Probably the Marquis meant to refer to Lady Jawjaw's marriage, which was to have taken place to-day.

Marquis M. M. That's it, that's it! She's laid up with an hysterical attack of the measles, and the honeymoon is to rise in the future.

Countess de F. A respite for his lordship.

Lady M. M. I should think he'd be so thankful, that he'd be almost willing tò have the small-pox.

Countess de F. Or have his intended mother-in-law die, so that out of respect for the corpse, the marriage might be indefinitely postponed.

Mabel. Well, now, they say he's dead in love with her.

Countess de F. I wonder if he's near-sighted. As it is said he has a positive dislike for intellectual women, this must account though for his great love for her. [*Enter Gabriel and Mr. B. Gabriel goes up and speaks to the Marquis in dumb show.*]

Mrs. B. [*Aside to Mr. B.*] What did you bring him here for?

Mr. B. To elope with you, though I might have known that even if you were willing he would n't be.

Mrs. B. Will you ever have sense?

Mr. B. You are always unreasonable. How can I be expected to have much, when my better-half has n't any?

Mrs. B. Did n't I beg of you not to recognize him, and above all not to bring him here?

Mr. B. I did n't bring him here, but he's welcome, nevertheless.

Mrs. B. [*With disdain.*] A poverty-stricken American!

Mr. B. So are you, for wisdom would not give ten cents' worth of stock to your name, if I did n't endorse the note. Do I object to this booby of a Marquis who is forever hanging around here, and who lacks in everything but the devil's accomplishments and dissipations.

Mrs. B. Booby! Well, it's not my fault if you don't know a gentleman from a booby. Then you didn't invite him here?

Mr. B. No, but since he's turned *valet* to your gentleman, I presume he's free to come and go with him.

Mrs. B. Oh! well, then, that accounts for his presence. I knew there had been some talk about his being the Marquis' valet, but did n't know such an arrangement had been made. [*Gabriel gives the Marquis a letter, which he opens and reads.*]

Gab. H. [*Aside.*] Yes, I see the story of my poverty makes the old lady as cold-looking as a two-year-old corpse, and Laura — well 'tis but the way with these women, — they're nervous, hysterical and heartless, and only measure a man by his bank account, and the fixings to his name. However, I'm satisfied that I've learned so soon what she is, for now I can account for myself. [*Looks at her.*] What a fool I was to allow that story to go uncontradicted, and further indulge in the whim of being this man's valet, just to get into her presence. I might have known that by such a course, I would n't get a nod, not to say a smile from her.

Marquis M. M. [*Aside to Gabriel.*] See here, did you know this was a challenge? [*Gabriel does not hear, but still looks at Laura.*]

Gab. H. [*Aside.*] Well, at least I can make it hot for this conglomeration of follies, and try to get even with his mother for daring to offer me such a position.

Marquis M. M. [*Aside to Gabriel again.*] Look here, did n't you know this was a challenge?

Gab. H. A challenge! No. [*All in chorus.*] A challenge!   .

Marquis M. M. Well, yes, now that it's out, it is an instrument of that nature.

Gab. H. It seems, Marquis, that some one has an ill-turn, and this is a bad symptom.

Countess de F. Who is it, Marquis, that has grown so careless of his life?

Marquis M. M. Lord Carra, it seems, has taken exceptions to the way his wife had fits in my presence the other night.

Countess de F. And so now wants to dry her tears by making her a widow.

Marquis M. M. And the funeral will take place precisely at seven.

Lady M. M. I supposed he had got over that fit.

Countess de F. I presume he's been waiting for his wife to get over hers, before he would indulge in his.

Marquis M. M. You might know he's a married man, or he'd never want to fight a duel with me.

Gab. H. Then suppose we go at once and accept everything, before our sober second-thought makes cowards of us.

Marquis M. M. Yes, we'll make him feel that he's been courting the inevitable — slapping fate in the face.

Gab. H. Certainly, being a nobleman, he should be satisfied to his heart's content. [*Exit Gabriel, followed by Marquis.*]

Mrs. B. And will this affair really terminate in a duel?

Lady M. M. Certainly, 'tis only a matter of blood now.

Mrs. B. A real live duel?

Lady M. M. I presume 'twill be lively, as they're both men of reputation.

Mr. B. [*Aside.*] I dare say, and poor reputation at that. [*The company gradually retire.*]

Mrs. B. [*To Mr. B.*] A duel! why bless me, this must be settled.

Mr. B. Certainly, that's what they propose to do when they meet. Do you suppose it'll be to express a silent contempt for each other?

Mrs. B. This is perfectly awful.

Mr. B. There, can't you let them fight in peace? This is no fuss of yours. Can't they mind their own business without your interference? What better use could either of them be put to than the object of a maudlin caravan? Do you suppose their friends wouldn't take pleasure in burying them?

Mrs. B. By all that's good, what's the matter with you? One would think to hear you talk, that you ought to be put in a padded room.

Mr. B. [*Aside.*] The cat's boiling in her. The cream of indignation's on her lips. [*To Mrs. B.*] Can't you let these people amuse themselves by getting us up a first-class mourning affair? Then when we return home we'll know how to grieve for our departed friends in the latest fashion. Now, if anything was to happen to me to-morrow, I should want you to turn out as if you knew how to dress, and have the hysterics as well as cry. Besides, you know, we haven't been in an aristocratic cemetery since we've been in France. What will folks say when we return home if we cannot boast of attending a high-toned funeral. Simply that we haven't been in fashionable society. Why, woman, don't you want to learn how to mourn in the most approved style? Do you suppose I am going to throw my money away and not learn to cry over you as becomes an affectionate husband, and above all a gentleman? There, shall it be the cemetery?

Mrs. B. I wouldn't go to one to-morrow if you were dead.

Mr. B. Very well, my dear; I hope to live long enough to return good for evil.

SCENE II.—*Discovered, Lady Max M. and Countess de F.*

Lady M. M. It must be confessed that the Marquis makes little or no impression on Miss Laura, though the old lady's admiration for him is evidently on the increase.

Countess de F. Perhaps she is of a romantic turn of mind and prefers a man of more robust character.

Lady M. M. Well, now, I had supposed him to be dissipated enough to please the most fastidious.

Countess de F. But undoubtedly she hears nothing about it, and if she does, her grandma won't let her believe it.

Lady M. M. She'd make a splendid match for him.

Countess de F. Certainly, and so to him you owe the best endeavors of a mother's wit. And to begin with, you've but to tickle the old lady's conceit a little to make her a most determined ally.

Lady M. M.   Oh! I'm well aware that we can depend on her, for she puts down his worst failings as eccentricities, in perfect harmony with his noble character and all that, — but to stimulate an ardent attachment for him in the young lady is quite another affair.

Countess de F.   Then, by the way, why not try her by having circulated a few harmless stories, making him out to be the dear profligate of your tears and fears, the hero of innumerable intrigues, love quarrels, duels, and, if need be, murder.

Lady M. M.   Yes! but his friends, knowing better, would be just mean enough to deny them.

Countess de F.   Suppose they do; we can manage it so that, at least in her estimation, they'll have an air of probability.   Then, you know as well as I, that nothing will open the eyes of most young ladies, and enable them to see the numerous hitherto undiscovered good points in a man's character, like some such a recommendation.

Lady M. M.   I can't see but that it would be the wisest thing a parent could do under the circumstances.

Countess de F.   Then all you've to do to charm her is to see that the stories are well-seasoned with a little scandal.   Indeed, I can't forget that I was young myself once, and that experience taught me that a young lady has great respect for a man whose character is not above reproach.

Lady M. M.   To be sure! In my time, as well as now, innocence was admired in its place, and that only in a baby.

Countess de F.   By the way, just to feel the young lady's pulse, how would it do to report him in some past intrigue with Lady Squib?   She, being dead, you know, can't contradict anything we say.

Lady M. M.   'Twould be better by far than to compromise the character of any living person, especially as the probability of her resenting it is out of the question.

Countess de F.   Besides, you know, we can have the stories contradict each other in such a way as to make it appear that some one was making desperate efforts to cover up the truth. This, no doubt, will interest her, and she may then think it but fulfilling her mission to fall in love with him, and by matrimony hope to reclaim him.

Lady M. M. But what about Mrs. Breeze?

Countess de F. 'Twill raise nothing but a good-natured suspicion in her, you can depend on it. In fact you'll probably find that such rumors will really prove a point in his favor with the old lady herself.

Lady M. M. After all, we'll have to be very careful with whom, in such reports, we ally his honor and good name.

Countess de F. Oh! certainly, 'twould never do in order to fascinate her and please the old lady, to go outside of the nobility with our stories, — though undoubtedly such a person as Mrs. Frothingham would just be delighted to have her name mixed up with some such noble scandal.

Lady M. M. There, I'll just call the Marquis and request him to remain at home till we return. [*Rings.*] Meanwhile, as I think very favorably of your plan, we can talk the matter over on our way. [*Enter servant.*] Tell the Marquis I wish to see him at once. [*Exit servant.*] But for the present, I only hope we can come to some understanding with Lady Carra about this threatened duel.

Countess de F. I'll warrant that after you make the necessary arrangements and pay her the amount agreed upon, that her lord and master will fight this duel according to her rules and regulations, for I really believe that if he undertook to have his own way in anything, she'd have one of her fits, to the great detriment of his hair.

Lady M. M. Well now, I thought he looked more bald after that last fit than I ever saw him before. I presume the poor man hopes that every fit will be her last. [*Enter Marquis in dressing-gown, slipshod, hair in disorder, eyes half shut, hands in his pockets.*] Why, Marquis, haven't you but just got up?

Marquis M. M. No, I've been up all night, but what's the rush?

Lady M. M. I want you to remain here till we return, as I expect to have news for you.

Marquis M. M. What's the matter? Another hysterical drive?

Lady M. M. I'll tell you when we return. Will you remain?

Marquis M. M. Yes, if you don't elope or meet somebody that father ought to fight a duel with.

Lady M. M. It's but a short drive, and we'll be back soon. [*Exit Countess and Lady M. M. Enter Gabriel.*]

Gab. H. So you're stirring, Marquis.

Marquis M. M. What do you mean, that I am trembling or shaking?

Gab. H. Oh! no; I mean that you're about.

Marquis M. M. About what?

Gab. H. Why, about your business. Well, as was understood in relation to Lord Carra's challenge, I've dropped his second, Col. De Lyon, a note last night, stating that as your second and humble servant, he'd find me here this afternoon.

Marquis M. M. When do you expect him?

Gab. H. At any moment.

Marquis M. M. The deuce! you haven't given me a chance to shave yet.

Gab. H. Don't mind it now; if anything happens, you know, you can be shaved afterwards.

Marquis M. M. Shaved afterwards! Why, you talk as if you confidently expected me to be the next inspiration for a funeral.

Gab. H. Well, as there is only one chance in two, there's no knowing but that you may be the next cause for a rise in crape.

Marquis M. M. Now oblige me, will you, by going beyond the grave with your possibilities.

Gab. H. Oh! no, let's leave that to the devil; but of course you mean to fight.

Marquis M. M. Fight? Certainly! Certainly fight. That that's done naturally is naturally the best thing that can be done.

Gab. H. You see if you come out of this scrape all right, with your nose pointing around the corner, or one of your eyes shot out, or one of Mars' warlike scars to decorate your noble brow, or your hair parted in the middle with a bullet, how it will enhance you in the estimation of that American young lady!

Marquis M. M. Ah! do you mean Laura?

Gab. H. Yes, and if the worst comes to the worst, you know, you won't have to die but once.

Marquis M. M. That's the worst of it; if I had to die twice, I wouldn't mind this once.

Gab. H. Oh! come, now, you don't mean to be a coward?

Marquis M. M. Coward! Coward! Do I look like a coward? Do I look like a fool deluded from his right mind? Yes, fight, if I can't stave it off. Under most any but the present circumstances, I would naturally, yes, naturally, like to fight, but now that I am about to engage in the great battle of life, that is, in getting married, my ammunition ought not to be thrown away on such an insignificant foe.

Gab. H. Then you intend to do all your fighting after you get married?

Marquis M. M. Well, I'd rather put it off till then.

Gab. H. May want to die then, hey?

Marquis M. M. Yes, or somebody else, but just now if I only could keep down my ire, I'd rather not fight, and won't, if we can manage to institute a stay of proceedings. I wish the old lady had stayed at home, — she could do this job up to the honor of the family.

Gab. H. She can't do it half as well as you can, Marquis, if you wouldn't be so bashful about running a fellow through.

Marquis M. M. I wouldn't mind fighting, I tell you, but when I think of the dear girl's love, why, I feel as if I must live for her future happiness. You see we've set so much by each other and all that sort of thing, that I can't bear the thought of running any risk.

Gab. H. [*Aside.*] Marry him! Engaged! Thus ends my dream. [*Aloud.*] Then you're engaged to her?

Marquis M. M. No, not quite engaged, but then she's looking me over, and I think I'll do, and I've no doubt but what I'll make a splendid specimen of a married man. I tell you, to become a woman's lord and master, is to assume a fearful responsibility, enough to deter a man of only ordinary courage.

Gab. H. I should think you'd almost rather fight a duel and take your chance, than to enter matrimony.

Marquis M. M. Well, that's the way a coward might look at it, but then sometimes it becomes a man to be courageous.

Gab. H. So you'll not fight?

Marquis M. M. Fight! I'll fight if I know myself, but the fact is, this duel must, for the time, be indefinitely postponed.

Gab. H. Then I'm to tell the Colonel that if his Lordship wants to fight, he'll have to pick a duel with some other fellow, as your time is worth too much to stop and butcher hogs.

Marquis M. M. No, no; I want to give his Lordship a chance to get out of this affair honorably. I'm not the man to take a mean advantage of another.

Gab. II. And you want to get out of it honorably, too?

Marquis M. M. Yes, anything rather than take a dishonorable advantage of a fellow's weakness.

Gab. H. Then there's only one thing for you to do.

Marquis M. M. What's that?

Gab. H. Be sick.

Marquis M. M. Sick! sick! with what?

Gab. H. Oh, with anything; a bottle of whiskey if you like.

Marquis M. M. And you'll tell him?

Gab. H. That you're sick. Yes, and so you are, lovesick, you know. So before the Colonel arrives, just lie down, and I'll send for the doctor at once.

Marquis M. M. What! be sick on an empty stomach? Isn't that dangerous?

Gab. H. There, you just lie down, and I'll order the doctor and your breakfast at the same time.

Marquis M. M. What doctor will you send for?

Gab H. For this Dr. Craft, who, you know, makes a specialty of midwifery.

Marquis M. M. But what are you going to say is the matter with me?

Gab. H. We'll leave that for him to find out, but if you're not satisfied, while I'm gone you can just step out and let a dog bite you, and then by the time he gets here we'll have a real, professional case of hydrophobia for him. Ah, I have it now. [*Goes to a case and brings out a bottle and glasses.*] There, can't you just start the *delirium tremens?* If you only have it as you did the last time, it'll be no case of humbug, either. [*Noise without.*] Who's that? [*Looks out of the window.*] Be off, Marquis; here comes Mr. and Mrs. Breeze, and their grand-daughter.

Marquis M. M. Can't I be sick after they go? You know they might catch it.

Gab. H. This is very fortunate; I'll tell them that the ladies are out, and that you're sick. You see we want to have it reported that you're sick before the Colonel gets here.

Marquis M. M. Well, I must say this is a sudden attack. [*Exit Marquis.*]

Gab. H. Now, while they are coming in, I'll drop a note to the doctor. [*Sits down and writes, then rings; enter servant.*] Here, take that to Dr. Craft, at once. [*Exit servant. Exit Gabriel, who immediately re-enters, followed by Mr. and Mrs. Breeze and Laura.*] I am sorry to say, Madame, that the ladies have gone out for a drive.

Mrs. B. So they're out, then?

Gab. H. Yes, Madame, they generally take their drives *out*.

Mr. B. [*Aside.*] Good, couldn't have done it better myself.

Mrs. B. I presume you're an old servant of the family?

Gab. H. Not so old, Madame; I'm only twenty-five.

Mrs. B. I mean long in their service.

Gab. H. Well, yes, for the last three weeks.

Mrs. B. [*Aside.*] Rather sharp, I must say. [*To Gabriel.*] I presume you've found your mistress to be a most excellent woman?

Gab. H. Oh! yes, she has a temper that would surprise a madman, a tongue like a loose jib in a gale, and a mouth like a steel trap, forever on the snap, a form like a barrel of soft soap on a stool, topped off with a pumpkin, and *feet* — stand her on her head and they'd answer for an umbrella. She's a good linguist of discord, a fashionable god-worshipper, ignores the devil and poor preachers, and is charitable with nothing but advice and lingo. She'd haggle with a butcher over a bone, or discharge a servant, if found smelling of a wine cellar, for being drunk; but with her many faults, she has a few virtues,— for instance, she's very dyspeptic, hysterical and nervous, and sometimes borders on insanity; then her hearing is impaired, caused, it is said, by a servant running a stick through a keyhole which brought up in her head; and she squints badly, the result, no doubt, of winking too much in her young days; then she's troubled with bunions, chilblains, catarrh, chapped lips, hangnails and a polypus in her nose, and she has a bad eruption of crusta lactea on her head, caused by drinking milkpunch, they say.; besides, she is full of nightmares, and as a somnambulistic pedestrian she makes the best show on record.

Mr. B. There, now that you've made her out to be quite a lady, perhaps you'll inform us what kind of a gentleman the head of the house is.

Gab. H. Oh! he's nothing but an aristocratic booby, a big fiddle that anyone can play on with a bottle of wine, a creation made for no direct purpose, except it is to be in the way and keep in vogue the word bore. In fact, he's a standing denial that his wife's a widow, a kind of a necessary tag to her being called Mrs. He figures well at the table, snores well in bed, and sees the bottom of the wine-glass oftener than any other man in the empire.

Mrs. B. Then, in your estimation I should judge they were well matched.

Gab. H. Well, one would know if he saw them together, that they were man and wife, and I rather think they have improved on all domestic dissensions.

Mr. B. It's no wonder her first husband died.

Mrs. B. Indeed! And is this her second abomination?

Gab H. Yes, this is her second victim, and I should judge, by her love for him, that she'd have the pleasure of weeping a widow's tears over even another husband's grave.

Mrs. B. [*Stiffly.*] May I ask, sir, what your position is here?

Gab. H. Certainly, Madame, certainly. [*A pause.*]

Mrs. B. Then, what is it?

Gab. H. Oh, a kind of tutor, governess or something of that nature, to the Marquis.

Mrs. B. That, I presume, includes waiter and barber.

Gab. H. No, Madame, but if it did, the man who feeds an ass and rubs him down, does nothing that makes him a being inferior to the ass.

Mrs. B. I presume you are ready to vouch for all you say?

Gab. H. To be sure, Madame! If ever I lie, it is in defending a good cause, and not a bad character.

Mrs. B. I'll remember and compliment your master that he has such a tongue as yours to noise abroad his qualities.

Gab. H. Not master, Madame, *protegé,*— but I fear your compliments will be thrown away on him, for he is not a person who appreciates a good thing.

[*Mr. and Mrs. B. going.*] *Mrs. B.* He'll not be without a character while he has you in his service.

Gab. H. [*Bows.*] Right, Madame, I've served his character many a turn. Since he's had me he's been in reputation. [*Exit Mr. and Mrs. B., followed by Laura.*]

Gab. H. If I haven't knocked her idol down, I've staggered him, to say the least. [*Exit Gabriel, enter Marquis.*

Marquis M. M. Well, if I'm going to be sick, it's about time for me to begin. I wonder what kind of sickness I'd better have. [*Re-enter Gab. H., followed by a waiter, who has the Marquis' breakfast on a tray, which he places on the table. Exit servant.*]

Gab. H. How you tremble.

Marquis M. M. Yes, I feel cold.

Gab. H. Then just lie down and let me cover you up at once. A cold mixed up with this sickness might result fatally, you know. [*Steps out, brings in some blankets and covers him up.*]

Marquis M. M. By Jove, Gabriel, this is being sick with a little comfort.

Gab. H. [*Takes the bottle.*] Now for something to warm you up. [*Fills a glass.*] Here's hoping your sickness will be a success. [*Drinks.*]

Marquis M. M. Do you expect to warm *me* up in that way?

Gab. H. Certainly, how can I make it hot for you if I'm not warmed up myself. [*Shoves the bottle and glass over to the Marquis.*]

Marquis M. M. [*Drinks.*] By the way, Gabriel, you know how nice and white a corpse looks, that's been bled to death?

Gab. H. Yes.

Marquis M. M. Well, suppose you touch me up a little with my make-up there, don't you think 'twould make a vast improvement on my sickness?

Gab. H. By all means, and if you were black around the eyes and foaming at the mouth, there'd be no doubt about your condition. [*Exit Gabriel, and returns with a toilet-box.*] We must do this up so as to make truth doubt's scarecrow. [*He blackens the Marquis around the eyes with hair dye, reddens his nose, and powders his face white all over; stands back and looks at him.*] Ghosts and goblins! you look as if you had been scared to death and buried for a year.

Marquis M. M. [*Sits up.*] But you don't get a grave-yard flavor from me yet, do you?

Gab. H. Oh, no, you smell just as sweet as you look, so lie down [*lays him down gently*], and keep covered up, and if you don't, you know you might have a relapse of something.

Marquis M. M. You see [*takes a drink*], all I want is just to make a sure thing of this sickness.

Gab. H. Then suppose I look you up a Chinaman nurse who has the leprosy,— come to think of it, you'd make a good leper.

Marquis M. M. Never mind the Chinaman, you're bad enough without mixing up any humbug with the matter.

Gab. H. Suppose you have the small-pox, then, and give it to everybody, especially Lord Carra, and by the way, you might pit him badly, say six feet under ground.

Marquis M. M. I respect the wholesale interest you have in leprosy, and take some stock in your taste for small-pox, but what I want is, that 'twill be generally known and appreciated that I'm sick, say with water on the brain.

Gab. H. But look here, everybody knows you never drink water.

Marquis M. M. Then you can say I tried some with such a bad result.

Gab. H. All right, we'll put it down water on the brain, and you can depend on me that I'll have your sickness come out in all the morning papers.

Marquis M. M. [*Takes a cigar out of his pocket.*] There, Gabriel, just light me a match, will you? [*Gabriel lights a match.*] Hold on to it now for about five minutes. Do you think there's a good chance for me to get out of this affair honorably?

Gab. H. By all means. It will add to your reputation as a fighter, duellist, man of honor, ladies' man, and above everything else, a nobleman. Hark! [*They listen. A voice without.*] Yes, that's the doctor's voice. [*He dumps the contents of the tray into the basket, then rings the bell violently. Re-enter servant, followed by Dr. Craft. To the servant.*] Bring me a pail of salt with a little water in it, also a mustard poultice made of everything that's hot in the house. Meanwhile bring me a glass of water for his feet, and a jug of brandy to stimulate him. [*Exit servant.*] There, Doctor, I think you'll find him just alive, and that's all.

Dr. Craft. Well, Marquis, how long have you been in this condition?

Marquis M. M. Ever since I've been sick.

Dr. Craft. [*To Gabriel.*] Did you give him anything?

Gab. H. Yes, gave him all the liquor I could find and followed it with an emetic.

Dr. Craft. [*Feeling the Marquis' pulse.*] Of what?

Gab. H. Soap and water, enough, by Jove, to make a bubble as large as the universe.

Dr. Craft. Did it act promptly?

Gab. H. Yes, he acted like an hydraulic ram, and

after sticking his head in this basket was soon relieved. [*Takes a lobster out of the basket.*] It's no wonder he was threatened with the scarlet fever, is it? [*Lays the lobster on the floor.*]

Dr. Craft. Why, has he shown any symptoms of that trouble?

Gab. H. Well, yes, just before that emetic worked, he was scarlet in the face. [*Takes a cold roast chicken out of the basket.*] It's surprising he hasn't had the chicken-pox, isn't it? [*Lays the chicken on the floor.*]

Dr. Craft. Yes, or an enlargement of the stomach.

Gab. H. [*Takes a large piece of corned beef out of the basket.*] It's no wonder the poor fellow came near being corned, is it?

Dr. Craft. If he had he'd have got into a pickle.

Gab. H. [*Lays the corned beef on the floor, and takes a pair of dumb-bells out of the basket.*] This, I presume, accounts for his being dumb for a short time.

Dr. Craft. Been indulging in dumb-bells then?

Gab. H. [*Lays the dumb-bells on the floor.*] 'Twas a mistake; he took them in the dark for pills. Didn't you take some pills, Marquis?

Marquis M. M. Yes, by the way I feel, I think I did, come to think of it.

Gab. H. [*Takes a live pup and kitten out of the basket.*] There, Doctor, can't you account for his symptoms of hydrophobia by these twins?

Dr. Craft. Has he had hydrophobia, then?

Gab. H. Oh! yes, but in a mild, tearful manner.

Dr. Craft. How is it that he happened to indulge in so much animal food?

Gab. H. Naturally enough; he thought they were game, and just took them down, and didn't know the difference till it was cat and dog with them in his stomach. [*Puts the pup and kitten facing each other on the floor, then dumps the contents of basket on floor, which consists of dishes, bottles, biscuits, doughnuts, cucumbers, corkscrews, &c.*] There, there, there isn't any use in going into details; you of course know what's the matter with him now.

Dr. Craft. Certainly; how do you feel now, Marquis?

Marquis M. M. Don't feel anything now.

Dr. Craft. What, don't you feel sick?

Marquis M. M. Oh! yes, I feel sick enough; I forgot that.

Gab. H. Well, Doctor, I presume you can now give me a certificate to the effect that he has the brain fever?

Marquis M. M. Water on the brain.

Gab. H. Hear the poor fellow, how he raves. It might be useful, you know, in case he was invited to court on the emperor's birthday.

Dr. Craft. Brain fever! He hasn't the brain fever.

Marquis M. M. Water on the brain.

Gab. H. I should like to know what this raving means if it's not brain fever.

Dr. Craft. [*Feeling the Marquis' head and pulse.*] My dear sir, there's no brain fever about him.

Gab. H. I should like to know who knows best, you or I.

Dr. Craft. Oh! you, to be sure.

Marquis M. M. Yes, it's brain fever, brain fever.

Gab. H. There, it is two to one that it's brain fever, and you know the majority rules.

Dr. Craft. Sir! was I called here to be insulted?

Gab. H. No, but to be convinced of the truth, and prescribe as we want you to, and that is to put it down brain fever. I should think you'd understand his case by this time.

Dr. Craft. [*Looks at Gabriel closely.*] I think I understand you now.

Gab. H. That's it, Doctor; if you comprehend me you understand the case perfectly.

Dr. Craft. Brain fever, at all hazards. [*Runs his hand over the Marquis' head.*] Well, now to be serious and leave joking to fools, I'm inclined to think that I believe, to say the least, that he is threatened with that complaint.

Gab. H. Brain fever will do nicely, Doctor,— put it down brain fever, and I'll swear you've got as near the truth as you ever did in all your life. [*Dr. Craft takes out a prescription book and writes. Hands certificate to*

Gabriel.] Thanks, Doctor. [*Reads.*] Brain fever; yes, that's what's the matter. [*Dr. Craft rises to go.*] How about his diet, Doctor?

Dr. Craft. Well, if he must eat pups, let them be cooked till the bark is taken out, and if kittens, why broil all the spit out of them.

Gab. H. Don't forget to send in your bill,— and by the way, is this fever catching? [*Exit Dr. Craft.*]

Marquis M. M. [*Sits up and takes a drink.*] It's enough to *make* a fellow sick to be clawed over in that fashion.

Gab. H. Yes, just as if you were a Bohemian candidate for the morgue, but after all I call him a good doctor.

Marquis M. M. Oh, he's a good doctor and all that, but he don't know his business; but look here, this is stupid work being sick. Here I am, and haven't had my breakfast yet.

Gab. H. That's according to Hoyle, you know we must starve a fever.

Marquis M. M. Well, you can starve the fever, but you can't starve me. [*Re-enter servant with card on tray, which Gabriel takes and reads.*]

Gab. H. Colonel De Lyon. Show him up at once. [*Exit servant.*] Now, Marquis, screw yourself up to the raving point, for he'll be here in a twinkling. [*Enter Colonel De Lyon.*]

Col. De Lyon. I presume it was your note I received last evening, stating that arrangements could be made with you to-day, for the meeting between Marquis Max Muddle and Lord Carra.

Gab. H. Yes, sir; I have the honor and pleasure.

Col. De Lyon. We are not alone, I see.

Gab. H. It's only the Marquis laid up with the brain fever, and for all I know it may turn into the small-pox, Asiatic cholera, or relapse into the leprosy or plague, for he's been very bad, seeming to have symptoms of everything. The doctors have all been here writing prescriptions, and disagreeing with great gusto and any amount of candor, but they all agree that if he lives nature'll have a job.

Col. De Lyon.   Now I'm very sorry he's sick, for if he had waited a day or two longer he might not have had to get sick in order to die.

Gab. H.   Well, now, I was thinking how fortunate it would be for his lordship if the Marquis wasn't well enough to meet him to-morrow.

Col. De Lyon.   Undoubtedly this is a very convenient sickness of his.

Gab. H.   Let me tell you sir, he'll meet his lordship to-morrow, small-pox or plague. You'll find, too, he can fight just as well sick as he can sober,— I mean well.

Col. De Lyon.   You know he has the choice of weapons.

Gab. H.   Oh, well, as for that, he can fight just as well with one weapon as another, and so can afford to be magnanimous, and allow his lordship the choice. Thus if his lordship had rather be run through than made the centre of gravity for a ball, we'll call it rapiers ; but if he'd rather be the mark for a deadly-aimed bullet, we'll make it triggers.

Col. De Lyon.   I'm not here to ask odds.

Gab. H.   We wouldn't consider it odds at all, only having some respect for a man's last request.

Col. De Lyon.   His lordship requests nothing but a meeting.

Gab. H.   Then his last request shall be gratified ; they shall meet.

Col. De Lyon.   At what hour shall it be?

Gab. H.   At four in the morning, unless his lordship would like to have affixed to the last few hours he'll ever sleep, an hour or two. He may have to cry with his wife for a while, you know, and that should be taken into consideration.

Col. De Lyon.   Well, sir, we'll try to accommodate him at four in the morning.

Gab. H.   Good ; and come to think of it, 'twill be just as well, for his lordship will get a good ways out of the world in two hours, and by that time, be over the chill of death, and begin to warm up a little.

Col. De Lyon.   Where shall they meet?

Gab. H.   At Fontainebleau, excepting his lordship prefers to die in some other locality.

Col. De Lyon. There, sir, we've had enough of this, —to-morrow at four. [*Exit Colonel.*]

Gab. II. Well, Marquis, don't you think I've arranged matters nicely?.

Marquis M. M. [*Gets up, angry.*] Oh, yes; want me to be butchered, don't you; think I'd make a good ghost and all that sort of thing. Fight to-morrow at four and be in hell at six. By all the blood of innocents ever shed, here I am to be butchered and roasted, and not a word to say about the matter, — and everything is arranged satisfactorily.

Gab. II. There, Marquis, you make me feel bad to hear you talk so.

Marquis M. M. Make you feel bad after making arrangements to have me in perdition at six to-morrow morning; and now there's no retreat but fight, and that's not my way of retreating. By all that's contagious, for what have I been sick?

Gab. H. Well, you see, I thought his lordship wouldn't want to fight a sick man; but when the Colonel referred to your sickness as being a convenient way to get out of this trouble, I just felt determined that his lordship should get all the fighting he wanted, if I had to meet him myself.

Marquis M. M. You take my place?

Gab. II. Yes, suppose I don your clothes, and you mine, and I go and meet him with you as my second. You know it will be scarcely light at four in the morning, and he'll not know me from you,— and in a short time, I'll promise you, he'll not know either one of us.

Marquis M. M. I like the idea.

Gab. H. So do I, and I should have thought that his lordship would have known that to challenge you would have been equal to committing suicide.

Marquis M. M. Nothing would delight me more than to meet this henpecked lord, and make the nymph of his palpitator shed crocodile tears and spoil crape over him.

Gab. H. Well, if you'd rather meet him yourself —

Marquis M. M. Oh, no; if it were not for other reasons, I'd stir my heart with ire, and make his wife the widow she wants to be; but as it is, I must not run any risk of blasting Laura's hopes by engaging in such a quibble.

Gab. H.   Let me see how we'd look in each other's clothes.   [*They exchange coats and hats.*]   Well, how do I look?

Marquis M. M.   Just handsome enough to bear me a dangerous resemblance ; but what kind of a show do I make?

Gab. H.   Oh! you look full of inspiration, determination, perspiration, and instigation.

Marquis M. M.   Well, that's about the way I feel.

Gab. H.   By the way, Marquis, you beat me all out, looking like a flunkey.   Then we'll meet his lordship in the morning?

Marquis M. M.   Well, if he's got to die, I don't see as 'twill save his soul whether he's killed by you or me. I owe his wife a grudge or I'd insist on killing him myself, but as it is you may only wound him, and so cheat her of her heart's desire.   [*Re-enter Lady M. M., Mrs. Breeze and Laura.   Lady M. M. rushes across room and throws her arms around Gabriel.*]

Lady M. M.   [*Kisses Gabriel again and again.*]   Why, my dear, what's the matter?   We met Mrs. Breeze here, who informed us that she called in our absence and found you sick and the doctor sent for.

Gab. H.   [*Aside.*]   This is a familiarity I never publicly allow.

Marquis M. M.   [*Faces the ladies.*]   I'm not very well.

Lady M. M.   [*Screams, starts back, and looks from Gabriel to the Marquis.*]   Monster! what does this mean?

Gab. H.   [*Looks at the Marquis as if he expected him to answer.*]

Lady M. M.   Mr. Hamilton, I am speaking to you.

Gab. H.   Excuse me, Madame, but you spoke so motherly, that I thought you were speaking to the Marquis.

SCENE III.—*Field and Forest Scene.   Enter Gabriel and Marquis, each dressed in the other's clothes.*

Gab. H.   Well, here we are, first on the ground. [*Takes out his watch and looks at it.*]   It is about time they were here.

Marquis M. M. Yes, and I hope they are not trifling with us.

Gab. H. You see his lordship is in no great hurry to face you.

Marquis M. M. He knows me by reputation, that's the reason.

Gab. H. By the way, Marquis, did your mother refer to this affair at all last night?

Marquis M. M. No, she commenced to tell me something, but we were interrupted, and I am glad of it, for she, like most women, always has something to tell me.

Gab. H. There they come. You're looking in the wrong direction. [*Slaps the Marquis' hat down over his eyes.*]

Marquis M. M. [*After fixing his hat.*] What's the matter? Do *you* want to pick a duel with me?

Gab. H. I only want to make them think, you know, that you got up savage this morning, ready to stick anything that's got blood in it. [*Knocks off the Marquis' hat, and gives him a kick.*]

Marquis M. M. [*Rubbing himself.*] I might as well stand up and be run through, as to be kicked to death by you.

Gab. H. Don't talk so loud, they'll hear you. It becomes a nobleman, you know, to kick his servant and knock him around; so you see every kick you get is a prop to your reputation, and of course we mustn't let it down for want of a few good props. [*Kicks him again, and trips him up.*]

Marquis M. M. [*Rubbing himself again.*] So you're going to kill me to prop my reputation.

Gab. H. Get up there and clear out, and I'll attend to this affair myself. [*Exit Marquis. Enter Lord Carra, and Col. De Lyon.*]

Col. De Lyon. I see I have the honor of addressing Marquis Max Muddle.

Gab. H. Well, sir!

Col. De Lyon. May I inquire for your second.

Gab. H. I have dispensed with him, and will attend to this business myself.

Col. De Lyon. [*Aside.*] I see he don't wish to have

nis second know that matters have been arranged as they are. [*To Gabriel aloud.*] Well, I presume, sir, you are aware that it has been agreed upon, between your and Lord Carra's friends, that you meet, and——

Gab. H. [*With dignity.*] It has been suggested, but I scorn the proposition.

Col. De Lyon. Indeed, sir, you astonish me; I thought you had agreed to it.

Gab. H. I have agreed to nothing but this meeting.

Col. De Lyon. But the friends of both of you concluded that between two such gentlemen as yourselves, a peaceful reconciliation should take place,—one that will do honor to your good names.

Gab. H. And so you and his lordship's friends get me up here at this time in the morning, and not even give me a chance to warm up a little. By Jove, sir, that's very unkind of you.

Col. De Lyon. Why can't you make a few friendly passes at each other, and express yourself satisfied?

Gab. H. I shall only ask for a few passes to express myself satisfied, I can assure you.

Col. De Lyon. Let me appeal to your honor to put by your passion.

Gab. H. Well, then, I'll smother it, and run him through as coolly as possible.

Col. De Lyon. I see you are inexorable. [*Crosses to Lord Carra, and talks in dumb show. Lord Carra advances, and looks Gabriel in the face.*]

Lord Carra. Do you mean to tell me that this is the Marquis?

Col. De Lyon. Certainly.

Lord Carra. This fellow is that valet of his.

Gab. H. Yes, and I am here to fill his place; I presume you can construe that.

Lord Carra. Sir, your master is a fool and coward.

Gab. H. Let him be what he is. I am here to make good that you are the prince of asses, if he has taken the liberty of calling you such.

Lord Carra. Bah! I don't fight with flunkeys.

Gab. H. No, I see you'd rather fight with a coward, or a fool worthy of your steel.

Lord Carra. [*As if going.*] Tell your master that I'll post him as a coward.

Gab. H. I dare say you can do that better than fight.

Lord Carra. Flunkey, go your way. If you were worth sticking, you'd be bleeding now.

Gab. H. Come, if you will argue, let it be with less talk.

Col. DeLyon. If the Marquis wasn't a coward, he would never have sent a servant to fight his battles.

Gab. H. Egad, for gentlemen, you don't think much of insulting a man behind his back, and a sick man at that.

Lord Carra. Sick!

Gab. H. Yes, sick; but I presume you would just like to fight a sick man.

Lord Carra. Sick! Sick!

Gab. H. Yes, sick; and here's the physician's certificate to prove it.

Lord Carra. It requires but a trifle to buy such.

Gab. H. But you must remember that this didn't come from the same one who gave out the report that you had the brain fever when down with the *delirium tremens.* [*Exit, Lord Carra, followed by Col. De Lyon.*]

Gab. H. I say, Marquis, where are you? [*Re-enter Marquis.*]

Marquis M. M. [*Looks around suspiciously.*] So they're gone.

Gab. H. By Jove, Marquis, you stood it well. Indeed, I never half appreciated your valor before.

Marquis M. M. I wish he was here now; I'd make hell gape for him.

Gab. H. That is, being a brimstone candidate, you'd elect him.

Marquis M. M. Yes, and I'd prove a faithful constituent.

Gab. H. There, Marquis, this will never do, and I've just thought of it. [*They exchange coats and hats rapidly.*] Your good name is eclipsed by the inspiration of a foul mouth. The honor of your ancient house is the roosting-place of insults, and so you must now fight or go down to posterity with your thumb in your mouth. So fire up, man, and hitch a span of dragons to your fury, while I bring him back to be trampled beneath your feet. [*Exit Gabriel in the direction taken by Lord Carra.*]

Marquis M. M. Honor! Rapiers! Fight! Blood! Funeral! Ghosts! Hell! I wonder if I could get honorably lost somewhere around here. [*Looks around and follows Gabriel. Re-enter Gabriel and Col. De Lyon.*]

Gab. H. Where is his lordship?

[*Col. De Lyon.* [*Looks back.*] Ah, there he is, talking with the Marquis, and shaking hands with him.

Gab. H. I see, the dog is trying to find out whether his Lordship trembles, or is in a cold sweat. [*Re-enter Marquis and Lord Carra arm in arm.*]

Col. De Lyon. There, gentlemen, this looks like an honorable reconciliation.

Gab. H. I deny it. Aren't they in arms against each other?

Col. De Lyon. Now, gentlemen, for the honor of your good names, suppose you make a few friendly passes at each other, and then we'll all breakfast together at the Hotel de Paris.

Gab. H. Yes, Marquis, and when you pass, remember that this is the man who took the liberty of calling you a coward.

Col. De Lyon. You forget that they are now reconciled.

Gab. H. Why, his lordship can't possibly be reconciled to a fool.

Marquis M. M. Fool?

Gab. H. Yes, he called you a fool.

Marquis M. M. He was only fooling then.

Gab. H. He said he would post you as a coward.

Col. De Lyon. Sir, 'tis now understood that this affair is to terminate to the honor of both these gentlemen. So now, my friends, to your places. [*They take their places, and the Colonel gives them the rapiers. They cross weapons, exchange a few passes, when the Marquis makes a near thrust at his lordship.*]

Gab. H. Look out, Marquis, you'll hurt him if you do

that again, and you know 'twould not be honorable to
fight this kind of a duel and draw blood.   [*While parry-
ing, each wounds the other in the hand.   They both drop
their rapiers.*]

Lord Carra.   Fury, man!   You've wounded me.

Marquis M. M.   [*Dancing around.*]   Fury don't half
express it.   Here's my hand probed to the core.

Lord Carra.   Beg pardon, 'twas not intentional, I can
assure you.

Marquis M. M.   You are the last person in the world
whom I would purposely hurt.   [*Marquis sits down and
holds his wounded hand with the other.   Lord Carra sits
on the stump of a tree.   In rushes Lady Carra, followed by
Lady M. Muddle, Mr. and Mrs. Breeze.*]

Lady Carra.   I told you, we'd be sure to find them
here.

Lady M. M.   True enough.   [*To Gabriel.*]   And
have they really been fighting?

Gab. H.   Yes, madam, they have been mutually prick-
ing each other.

Lady M. M.   [*Rushes to the Marquis and throws her
arms around him.*]   Oh! horror, horror, they have killed
my poor boy.

Mrs. B.   Dear me, there's no depending on a duel.
Some one is just as likely to get hurt as not.

Lady M. M.   Oh, dear, see the horrible blood.

Marquis M. M.   Yes, but I am only wounded in the
—— [*Attempts to rise.*]

Lady M. M.   No, no, you mustn't attempt to rise.

Marquis M. M.   But I'm only wounded in——

Lady M. M.   My dear! my dear, you musn't attempt
to get on your feet in this condition.   I'll have you put
on a stretcher, and taken to my carriage at once.

Marquis M. M.   But I'm only wounded in the——

Mrs. B.   Just like these men.   I really believe they'd
walk to their funerals if they got a chance.

Lady M. M.   Hamilton, don't you think you could
find something at yon farm-house, that would do for
a stretcher?

Gab. H.   I can see.   [*Exit Gab.*]

Lady Carra. [*To Lord C.*]   Well, are you almost gone?

Lord Carra. [*Jumps up excitelly.*]   Not by all the widows in France.

Lady M. M. [*To Marquis.*]   Yes, my dear, I've been looking for you all night.

Marquis M. M. For what did you want me?

Lady M. M. To speak to you about this affair, before it took place.

Marquis M. M. Can't I fight a duel without being bothered about it?   [*Re-enter Gab. with the stretcher.*]

Lady M. M. Yes, 'twas an all-night hunt for you.

Gab. H. [*Aside.*]   And through my good management he couldn't be found.

Mr. B. [*Aside.*]   Just the thing to carry a man on who has a sore finger.

Lady M. M. We'll just put him on it, and take him at once to my carriage. [*Gab. helps the Marquis on the stretcher.*]

Gab. H. There Mr. Breeze, suppose you just give me a lift. [*They carry him a few steps when the stretcher breaks, and he falls on the stage.*]

Marquis M. M. You must let me walk, I'm only wounded in the—— [*Exit Marquis.*]

[QUICK CURTAIN.].

ACT III.

SCENE I. — *Drawing-room in the Breezes' apartments.
Discovered Mr. and Mrs. Breeze.*

Mrs. B. Oh! If I were a man, I'd have my wife's
love, children's fear, friends' respect, and enemies'
hate.

Mr. B. Seeing you can't conveniently be a man, you
ought to be proud of being the wife of your ideal of a
man.

Mrs. B. My ideal! A being as full of follies as he
is of infirmities.

Mr. B. Well, my dear, at least I have been a husband.

Mrs. B. Ah, yes, circumstances so controlled you;
society so calls you, but your own conscience denies it.

Mr. B. You haven't grown thin on it, my love.

Mrs. B. And so you'll sit there,— oh, if I could make
you have a little sense, my talking might amount to
something.

Mr. B. So this is for what you wanted me to spend
the evening at home?

Mrs. B. 'Twas to have a sensible talk with you.

Mr. B. Then, my exquisite, it's about time for you
to begin.

Mrs. B. I wanted to speak to you about Laura's matrimonial prospects.

Mr. B. Take my advice and let Laura do her own
wooing and cooing. Nobody ever made a match for
you, when you married me, and I'm sure you could never
have done better, if all the match-makers in the country
had been working in your interest.

Mrs. B. I see; to have your grandchild properly
wedded, and not make the mistake that I did, is a matter
of no consequence to you.

Mr. B. Properly wedded! That's blood, blood,
blood, and you look for blood among these pale ghosts?

Mrs B.　Do you want her to marry a negro?

Mr. B.　Oh no, but a lord, earl or prince. If she can't do any better, I presume you wouldn't object to a king, for her.

Mrs. B.　There's the Marquis, for instance.

Mr. B.　Yes, there he is, as you say, for instance.

Mrs. B.　Well, isn't he of noble blood, and for what more could she wish? Isn't he a man, and above all, isn't he a Marquis?

Mr. B.　Yes, a Marquis, and that's just about the bulk of what he is.

Mrs. B.　Look at his reputation as a man of honor, and his valor in defending his good name.

Mr. B.　Do you refer to that mutual wounding affair he had with Lord Carra, the other day?

Mrs. B.　Yes, that's it. If he had died with a ball shot through him, you'd say he'd been scared to death. If you were a man of honor yourself, and a gentleman, you'd know better, perhaps, how to appreciate him. [*Turns away.*]

Mr. B.　[*Aside.*] If I were a man of honor and a gentleman! So I'm nobody, and he's a blooded gentleman and an honorable Marquis? Ah! suspicion! I have it; she's infatuated with him herself, and this makes truth out of the insinuations of the Countess de Foy, whom I accidently heard say, that while my wife pretends to court the Marquis for her grandchild, she woos him for herself, and manages the pretence well. Suspicion thickens. [*Exit Mr. B. hurriedly.*]

Mrs. B.　It's time the Marquis was here. [*Enter Gabriel.*]

Gab. H.　[*Assuming a cringing attitude.*] The Marquis sent me here in great haste to tell your ladyship that he would follow me as quick as an unexpected delay would permit; his compliments come with his excuses.

Mrs. B.　[*Aside.*] One might know his master was a gentleman for his servant is the master of good manners. [*To Gabriel.*] Well, my good man, do you know what has detained him?

Gab. H.　I know not, except that where he went there's more and better wine than you keep here. He said, "Let's cut our visit by an hour, for what's the use of swapping ideas for half a day with a grim, gray, and sixty-year-old hag?"

Mrs. B. [*Aside.*] I'm just sixty, but even Breeze don't know that by half a dozen years. [*To Gabriel.*] Did he refer to his coming here to see me, when he spoke in that manner?

Gab. H. He didn't speak of you or of coming here at all, my lady, he only said she, and he knows she's enough. He spoke not of you when he said "She's a skinflint, with her virtue." He said they both were asses, the one an old ass, and the other a young one. Now, he had no thought of you when he spoke thus, for he knows a donkey from an ass, he does; he's very sharp about such things, my lady.

Mrs. B. Impudence! Do you mean to insult me? Did your master call me and my granddaughter asses that you might come and ape his insults here by calling me a donkey? Wretch! what do you mean?

Gab. H. I beg your mercy's pardon if I have offended. My master did not say that you were asses, and if he did, would I make a liar of him by calling you a donkey. No, my lady, you're not an ass nor yet are you a donkey. My master said she was a virtuous wife; now he would never think of saying that of you.

Mrs. B. Would he dare to say anything to the contrary?

Gab. H. Dear lady, my master is a gentleman, a virtuous gentleman of gentle blood. Now, you're a lady, a virtuous lady, a lady of gentle blood.

Mrs. B. [*Aside.*] Now he knows what he's talking about.

Gab. H. Such being the case, the Marquis would not and could not talk so of you. He said her wit was no match for her tongue, and that she liked her beer. Now I take it that if he meant you, your nose gives him the lie, for it looks as white as if it were powdered.

Mrs. B. [*Gets irritated, and walks up and down the room, knocking over a number of articles. Aside.*] If I get angry with the booby, I'll not learn what he knows concerning the stories I've heard about the Marquis. [*To*

Gabriel.]   See here, my man, is there any truth in these tales that are going around about your master?   [*Enter Laura.*]

Gab. H.   Well, if the Marquis does love dogs, and puts them on the foxes' trail, and follows after on a bob-tailed nag, or if a mishap ducks him in a brook, or rolls him in a bog, a dirty lump, bear you in mind he is of gentle blood.   If he fights cocks and dogs, and bets at cards to make his passing hour enjoyment's time, and gives himself up to the gay dissipations of the night, to talk and songs, though lewd; to wine, though it be drank to shame all sense; to dance, though his half-nude partner, like himself, steps to the music of a drunken fiddle, — bear you in mind he is of gentle blood.   If anyone says he is out nights, so say I, are angels of mercy. If they say he goes to bed with his boots on, I say, he pays to have the sheets washed.   If they say he likes women, I say, so do I, and if women like him and me, why, it's no fault of ours that we were made for women's liking.   So bear in mind, when scandal puts her tongue out at him, that he is of gentle blood.   One whom for such reproaches you should find excuses; but were he a dirty cur and such a nuisance, there'd be some excuse in hanging him.   [*Mrs. B. turns away.   Exit Gabriel H.*]

Laura.   Some folks admire a man of marked reputation; now, for such, this Marquis has enough of it to worship.

Mrs. B.   Well, some of these young noblemen are just a little wild.

Laura.   And so, grandma, you'd like to see me this man's wife?

Mrs. B.   'Twould please me indeed to see you wed him.

Laura.   Why, grandma, such a character for a husband!

Mrs. B.   I'd rather see him as he is, young, wild and foolish, for were he wise, sedate, and over-exacting, no amount of worship would flame his heart.   Some day you'll be a lady, and then you'll thank me for my care and pains that shape your course so well.   Remember, love and kindness will tame wildness, and that riches and titles make love's nest cosy.

Laura. Though I have a love, 'tis not for him to slay,
With dissipation and its satellite abuses,—
No love to pet and win a profligate,
From tastes that are engrafted in his nature;
I have not two minds, whose visions conflict,
The one to behold the truth and feel its force,
The other to see a lie as its ideal,—
Or two hearts to judge, the one to belie the other;
Nor two loves, the one that abhors the thought of him,
The other that has all my nature's sweets for him.

Mrs. B. I tell you, girl, love's not what you suspect it,
Not what deceitful passion 'd teach you to believe;
You've lived a maid, till old enough to be a wife,
Now dedicate yourself to wisdom's best choice.
This thing the world calls love, this bait for hot passion,
That blurs the sight, and robs young folks of their senses,
Is kin to whooping-cough, chicken-pox, and measles,
And like them, too, it spends itself in one attack.
As you start out on this great journey of life,
Be wise, and take the guide who has feet to walk,
Who has eyes to see all objects in his path,
And a man's strength in his arms to lift you
O'er all pitfalls, where dwells bleak poverty;
Whose means will make your journey one of pleasure,
And leave you every sense free to enjoy
The world's varied scenery which will present itself.

Laura. Love is the link which binds our hearts in faith;
The ruling spirit of each sweet caress,
The dear companion of our life and hope,
The guiding thought of every day's bright dream,
Heaven's guardian angel of our honors,
The blest soul of every virtue. For him
I've scarce respect, speak not of love.

Mrs. B. Girl, do you intend to dispute my experience
In this matter of love, men, and marriage?
Have I studied their natures, whims, and follies
For twoscore years, and still not know them?

Have I twice been a bride, and yet to learn
That as many times I've been duped by them?
Have I not fathomed their souls for affection,
And for my trouble got the mud of their natures?
Do they not on their knees, with budding lips,
Heap vow on vow, and swear lies in love's language?
What bosh they babble out to every girl they hug;
The cream of nonsense lies hid in their tongue's charm.
Oh! when will women get their senses, and take them
For what they are, and not for what they say?

    Laura.   Men are not like strange animals in a far-off
    land.
Beyond our sight's and understanding's reach;
No, here they are, the knights of our civilization,
Our country's bulwark in the time of war,
Our gallants, and fair rulers in the time of peace,
Our fathers in our childhood's helpless days,
The husbands and companions of our married lives.

    Mrs. B. Girl, you're not old enough to know what
men are. Their deceit and conceit are measured alike.
The lowest institutions of our country are supported by
these our lords of creation; and yet their looks of virtue
win our maiden smiles, till we, poor trusting things, with
horror see them, in their real characters, beard-faced
hypocrites. Then they laugh, and say we're soft and
silly, and looking owlish, talk of wisdom's ways, with the
sense of parrot-talking school-boys. Their eternal prattle
needs no description, — 'tis money, women, politics, and
religion.

    Laura. Then, grandma, you can't think much of me
to wish me to wed one of them, and especially this one.

    Mrs. B. But with such as he, nature has blessed the
world for some woman's sake.

    Laura. I think it a matter of doubt that nature ever
had anything to do with him, and if she did, she certainly owes the world an apology.

    Mrs. B. Girl, go to your room, and remember that
he is my choice for your husband, and that I'm not to be
crossed in my purpose. [*Re-enter servant, who shows in
the Marquis. As the Marquis enters, Laura goes off.*]
Ah! Welcome Marquis, welcome. [*Mrs. B. advances to
meet him.*]

Marquis M. M. Madame, it pleases me to find you alone, for the delicacy of my situation involves much. [*Mr. B. puts his head in at the door.*]

Mrs. B. [*Laughing.*] Ah! Marquis, I've been treated to a recital of a few of your bad doings.

Marquis M. M. Indeed, madame, there's no laughing down what some folks say. I've tried it myself, and find they will tell the truth anyway, or lie at all hazards.

Mrs. B. Sure enough! Some folks do talk according to the rules and regulations of falsifying.

Marquis M. M. That isn't the worst of it;—they lie, too.

Mrs. B. True, scandal will have its victims, and morality its angels.

Marquis M. M. Suppose these people were to talk of you and me, would there be any truth in it?

Mr. B. [*Head in at the door.*] Folks talking about them already.

Mrs. B. Of course not. If they did, they'd only represent us in a false light.

Marquis M. M. Such lights should be put out.

Mr. B. [*Head in at the door.*] Put the light out?

Marquis M. M. My dear madame, I've been thinking as you've been very kind to me, that should I make advances in the right direction, they'd meet with your hearty approval.

Mrs. B. Certainly; you shall have my warmest considerations.

Marquis M. M. After all, I fear you will be flustrated as much as myself, when you hear what I am about to propose.

Mrs. B. Compose yourself, my dear Marquis, I'm not easily flustrated.

Mr. B. [*Head in at the door.*] My dear Marquis! What will it be next?

Marquis M. M. It's an awful thing to be in love.

Mr. B. [*Head in at the door.*] Yes, with another man's wife, it is fearful.

Mrs. B. Dear me, if the door isn't open all the time. Suppose we have it closed.

Marquis M. M. Yes, my idea of privacy exactly.

[*The Marquis rises and shuts the door.*] Well, madame, as I was about to remark, I think it high time I was blessing some one as a matrimonial superior.

Mrs. B. You know I have always looked on your suit with favor.

Marquis M. M. Yes, madame, I'm aware that I owe everything to your encouragement, but, is Mr. Breeze at all suspicious that I'm matrimonially interested in your granddaughter?

Mrs. B. I doubt that he has given the matter a thought.

Marquis M. M. Of course there'll be no serious objections on his part.

Mrs. B. Oh, no, he always finds it convenient for me to have my own way in everything.

Marquis M. M. Then I've nothing to fear from him.

Mrs. B. I thought I heard some one at the door.

Marquis M. M. So did I, perhaps there is. [*Marquis rises and opens the door, when in tumbles Mr. B.*]

Mrs. B. Why, goodness gracious, my dear, what's the matter?

Mr. B. [*Gets up in a fury.*] Oh! So you don't know? Lost your flustration, and want to know what the matter is. My dear Marquis,—and—it's an awful thing to be in love,—and you've always looked on him with favor,—and you must have the door shut, and put out the lights, and you've nothing but warm consideration for his advances, and he can depend on you in such an emergency, and *you* want to know what the matter is. So, woman, you've turned from me to that toadstool of humanity to prove how conspicuously depraved has become your taste.

Marquis M. M. Sir, may I presume,——

Mr. B. If you do, by Jove, I'll wring your noble neck. You presume,—and have the check not to sneak out of here like a cur. Get. [*Catches him by the coattails and collar of his coat, and pushes him toward the door, against Mrs. B. who stands with her back to the door.*]

Mrs. B. [*Hysterically.*] You brute! you brute! What does this mean? [*She locks the door and puts the key in her pocket.*] There, we'll have an understanding about this at once.

Mr. B. [*Releases the Marquis.*] Certainly, being a female combination of logical resources, I presume you think you can trump up some good excuse, but, believe me, woman, you've played your last card with me, you have put your finger in my eye just once too often. I may be a fool, but for this time I'll cover up my foolishness with a little wisdom.

Mrs. B. I wouldn't forget myself, my dear, and act so entirely unnatural.

Mr. B. Open that door.

Mrs. B. Sir?

Mr. B. Open that door, or I'll run your paramour through its panels.

Mrs. B. I'll not open it till you beg the Marquis's pardon for all this abuse.

Mr. B. Beg his pardon?

Mrs. B. Yes, and mine too; you've made a pretty lunatic of yourself this evening. Tut, man, what does all this mean?

Mr. B. Don't tut me, woman,—what does all this mean,—that I'm suspicious of this toot here,—and other things too bad and too numerous to mention,—no knowing how much more.

Mrs. B. Oh, you monstrosity of foolishness! What the Marquis asked was, if you were at all suspicious that he was in love with our Laura.

Marquis M. M. Yes, and I was just trying to find out whether you'd object to the honor of having me for a son-in-law or not.

Mrs. B. I undertook to tell you once this evening, that overtures had been made to me, by Lady Max Muddle, to bring about a marriage between our child and the Marquis here. But you got your senses so snarled up, that I thought it best to let you go and untangle them first.

Mr. B. [*Aside.*] I don't know but I've made a fool of myself.

Mrs. B. The idea of your rushing in here like a mad bull, fury wild, in quest of some phantom of your spleen.

Marquis M. M. Your wife's paramour? What do you mean, sir?

Mr. B. Oh, no, I'm not such a fool as to be jealous of you.

Marquis M. M. Sir, you insulted me.

Mr. B. Insulted you! Why, can't you take a joke? If ever you become my son-in-law, you must expect worse treatment than this. You must bear in mind, too, that in such a case, my wife here would become your grandmother-in-law.

Marquis M. M. Sir, I expect an apology.

Mr. B. But my Laura is no apology.

Marquis M. M. But you insulted me, sir.

Mr. B. Well; if I called you an ass, and you're not one, why, it's all the better for you. So you love our Laura, then.

Marquis M. M. Yes, considerably better than her grandfather.

Mr. B. How do you know? This, I know is a little inquisitive, but then there's nothing like having an understanding.

Marquis M. M. Well, I feel as if it wouldn't be a bad idea for me to get married.

Mr. B. It might not be bad for you, but how would it be for the girl you'd marry?

Marquis M. M. Oh! A splendid thing for her, I can assure you.

Mrs. B. Now you're talking and acting like sensible men. [*Enter servant.*]

Servant. Fire! Fire! The house is all on fire. [*Exit servant with haste. Smoke enters.*]

Mr. B. Now keep cool, till I find out where it is. [*Exit Mr. B.*]

Mrs. B. Keep cool in a fire? Just like him. [*They all rush out. Re-enter Mrs. B. and Laura. Smoke comes with them.*]

Laura B. I wonder if poor grandpa is safe.

- *Mrs. B.* Oh! I shall faint, I shall faint, and to be burned up in a faint is perfectly horrible. [*She staggers towards the door, and falls in a faint.*]

Laura B. Oh, heavens, isn't there any possible way to save her? I must call for help. [*Exit Laura.*]

Marquis M. M. [*Re-enters, and approaches Mrs. B.,*

whom he mistakes for Laura.] Here, Miss Laura, let me save you. [*He takes her up in his arms, and while attempting to carry her off, drops her repeatedly.*]

Mr. B. [*Re-enters with fire extinguisher on his back.*] The devil! Here they are hugging each other like wild-cats. [*He plays on them. The Marquis drops Mrs. B.*]

Marquis M. M. Look here, we're not on fire. [*Exit Mr. B, playing a stream of water in every direction. The Marquis now sees that instead of Laura it is Mrs. B. whom he is attempting to carry off.*] [*Aside.*] Why, this is only the granny. [*Aloud.*] Mrs. Breeze, excuse me, I mistook you for your granddaughter. Pardon my familiarity. Excuse me a thousand times, and I'll send a man to help you out if possible. [*Exit Marquis.*]

Mrs. B. [*Rises and follows him toward the door, stag-gering,—where she faints again. Enter Laura who gropes her way to the door, where she finds her grandmother. She stoops over her.*]

Laura B. Oh! Horror! Horror! Left to such a fate! [*Enter Gabriel.*]

Gab. H. 'Twas her voice I heard calling for help, and she seemed somewhere in this direction. [*While groping around he finds her.*] Let me take you from this place at once. [*Takes off his coat and rolls around her, and goes out with her in his arms. Cheers from without. Re-enters again with a long cloak wrapped about him, and again gropes around in the smoke until he finds Mrs. B.*] Ah, yes, here she is. [*Takes his cloak off, wraps it around her, and goes out with her in his arms. Cheers from without.*]

SCENE II.—*Drawing-room in Hotel. Discovered Countess de Foy and Lady Carra.*

Lady Carra. Then Mr. Hamilton told you the amount he received.

Countess de F. Yes, and I tacitly admitted that I sent it to him. I also learned from him that the check was cashed by the Bank de Paris, and further that Mr. Breeze's orders are cashed by the same bank. So you see suspicion would point to Laura as the person who sent him that money. [*Enter Laura with book in her hand. She sits down at a table.*] Well, Miss Bliss, have you become reconciled to your change of quarters?

Laura B. Quite so, and one meets so many friends at a hotel you know, that for a time, at least, it makes it very pleasant.

Countess de F. I wonder what has become of Mr. Hamilton. Why, I haven't seen him since the night of the fire.

Laura B. I presume he's still in Paris.

Lady Carra. Indeed, it's a mystery to me, how he maintains himself, now that he's no longer the Marquis's valet.

Countess de F. Without any trouble, I can assure you, while a certain female friend of his has a purse. [*Laura starts and Lady Carra and Countess de Foy look knowingly at each other.*]

Lady Carra. Ah! then 'tis a woman who with one hand on her heart, offers her purse to him with the other.

Countess de F. Certainly, and he knows 'twas but a bid for his love. [*They rise.*]

Lady Carra. I wonder how high she values it.

Countess de F. Oh! something like three thousand francs for a start.

Lady Carra. That must have been flattering to his vanity.

Countess de F. 'Twas a good offer for a bankrupt stock. [*They go up the stage, laughing, and looking back at Laura, and go off.*]

Laura. [*Rises.*] Then he knows all, and told *her* too, and that I have tried to buy his love. [*Exit. Re-enter Mrs. B. and Gabriel.*]

Mrs. B. Why, Laura said she'd remain here till I returned. Yes, Mr. Hamilton, we all have many thanks for you, — but to only thank you for saving my child's life, is far from my intentions. There, my dear sir [*holds out a purse*], allow me to present you with this purse as a token of our appreciation of your bravery, and believe me, while my eyes ever rest on the face of my child, I shall mentally thank you as the preserver of her life.

Gab. H. Thanks, madame, alone are acceptable.

Mrs. B. The purse is worthy of the deed.

Gab. H.   Then it contains your daughter's thanks.
[*Re-enter Laura.*]

Laura.   Here I am, grandma, to administer my own
thanks.   [*Holds out her hand, which Gabriel takes.*]
There, being mortal, what more can I do than thank you?

Gab. H.   Prevail on madame, here, to put up her
purse.

Mrs. B.   Then you refuse it?

Gab. H.   Your daughter's thanks, madame, have paid
me well.   [*Enter Mr. B.*]

Mr. B.   My dear, there's something wrong about these
French keyholes.   They are always in the wrong place,
and upside down when you find them.

Mrs. B.   Couldn't you get into your room?

Mr. B.   Oh, yes, if the door wasn't locked there'd be
no trouble about getting in.

Mrs. B.   [*Aside to Mr. B.*] I presume not, then you'd
fall in.

Mr. B.   Talk about falling, I just fell over a cat as
black as Lady Proudblood's character.   Yes, and when
I was looking at the chambermaid up stairs, you know,
the one with diamond black eyes, and lips as red as her
mistress' nose, and form that makes a fellow feel as
though he'd like to be a widower, with his arm about her
waist; well, I came near falling again, and would, if I
hadn't brought up against her.   Then, this maker of beds
had the audacity to tell me to go away, — that I was
drunk, — yes, woman, a female has insulted your lord and
master, the seal of your heart, the consolidated bond-
holder of your affections, the one to whom, you know,
you declare all their dividends.   [*Looks at her tenderly.*]
The inspiration to your genius for pet names, you know.

Mrs. B.   She did just right.

Mr. B.   Of course, I really believe if a person shot
me, you'd thank them for it.   Well, the impudence
of these servant girls can't be beat, except by their mis-
tresses.   If a man so far forgets himself as to act
civilly with them, they just practise their sauce on him,
and then his wife tells them to do it again, and she'll raise
their pay.

Mrs. B.   Let me see the key that you tried to unlock

your door with. [*Gives her a corkscrew.*] That, why that's a corkscrew, you——

Mr. B. Corkscrew! Let me see. [*She returns the corkscrew.*] True enough; who'd have thought you'd have been right for once?

Mrs. B. [*Takes him by the arm.*] There, let me see if I can unlock your door.

Mr. B. [*Just discovers Gabriel.*] By all that's combustible, if here isn't Mr. Hamilton. [*They advance and shake hands.*] There, my dear fellow, I'd rather shake your hand than any hand in Europe. [*Holds on to Gabriel's hand. Mrs. B. tugs at Mr. B.'s sleeve to get him to go.*] Yes, sir, that hand restored my little girl to me, — that hand snatched her from the flames that leaped before my very eyes. I feel that my heart isn't big enough to do you honor; but there, Mr. Hamilton, we shall meet again. As I feel tired now, I think I shall retire. [*Exit Mr and Mrs. B.*]

Laura. Mr. Hamilton, won't you be seated? [*Gabriel takes a chair.*] It seems, sir, that to only thank you for my life is but to be ungrateful, and not to rightly appreciate your noble bravery, and the fearful death from which you rescued me. But let me assure you that through the coming years of my life, memory will ever do you honor, and friendship hold you in high esteem.

Gab. H. Who wouldn't go through fire for such a reward, and be doubly thanked to see you safe, and though surrounded with beauty, lovely as the diadem that crowns it.

Laura. Please don't think me a child that you can flatter.

Gab. H. No, but a woman to whom I can speak the truth; a shrine where honest praise can do homage.

Laura. Thanks, the compliment is worthy of you.

Gab. H. [*Gets up and approaches her.*] Laura, — will you give me the right to call you Laura?

Laura. 'Tis a father's right, and I care not to be adopted.

Gab. H. 'Tis a husband's right. [*Laura rises.*]

Laura. Sir, did you save my life that I might pay you with my heart, though it should go a sacrifice?

Gab. H. Far from it. Could I win your love, I'd take it as a boon from Heaven ; but should you offer yourself as a sacrifice, you'd not be worth the taking. No, since first we've met, I've been possessed of love, and since, no moment's thought has been free of you ; no hope I've had that left you out.

Laura. [*Aside.*] And so, with perhaps a kiss of hers upon his lips, and French flattery on his tongue, he comes to me with hopes to win my love. [*To Gabriel.*] Sir, you saved my life ; for that, you have my thanks, and good gold has been offered you. You have the one, and still can have the other. But name your reward, and if my word prevails it will be yours. Don't stop to divide, but multiply. Dream not that I'll make my heart a sacrifice. No, far from it, for first I'd let it burn in my body. Though life is sweet, it is no equivalent for a life that tramples love, honor, hope, happiness, all beneath my feet. Yes, my heart and love are more than a price for my life. They have the value of every virtue that makes up the human soul.

Gab. II. 'Tis enough. By what I've heard, I knew it would be folly, madness, and yet love would have its fit. To-day, to-day you've crushed the fondest hope my heart has ever cherished. [*Exit Gabriel.*]

Laura. Now he can go back to his lady-love, convinced that that money of mine was no bid for his love ; and yet, I do love him, till it seems as if madness would be the result of refusing him. [*Takes out her handkerchief and bows her head in her hands. Re-enter Mrs. B. Laura looks up.*] Oh ! grandma, I wish you'd take me home ; I'm tired of Paris and all the world but home. [*Re-enter Countess de Foy and Lady Carra.*]

Countess de F. And Miss Laura is tired of Paris? Why, my dear, you haven't even tasted its sweets yet,—and Paris, you know, is the world's honey-comb of pleasure, and when once you've learned to love it, no ties can win you from it.

Mrs. B. There, my dear, I think you'd better come to your room, at once. This is only a re-action from the late excitement at the fire. [*Exit Laura and Mrs. B.*]

Countess de F. It's too bad about the poor thing,

isn't it? I presume she's never been further in a love affair before, than to admire herself. [*Re-enter Gabriel.*]

Gab. H. My lady, I was just on the point of leaving the hotel, and wishing to see you privately for a moment, I thought, if agreeable to you, the present time was as good as any.

Lady Carra. Then I think I may be excused for the present.

Countess de F. Oh, certainly; but what in the world, Mr. Hamilton, possessed you to make Miss Laura weep?

Gab. H. And was she really in tears?

Countess de F. [*Laughing.*] Tears! Yes, hysterical tears, such as women often shed after laughing too much. But what a magnificent creature she is, to be sure.

Gab. H. She is, indeed, a beautiful woman.

Countess de F. Yes, and modest enough to cheat the most suspicious, and then, you know, she should be encouraged for trying so hard to be a lady.

Gab. H. She is a lady,

Countess de F. Indeed, I did hear that a dissipated nobleman almost threw himself away on her, but nothing more. If she's *not* married to one, I wouldn't be surprised to hear of her making some such a matrimonial alliance, for her dear grandma is determined to make a lady of her, though the metamorphosis of making her one should be performed even by a monstrosity.

Gab. H. It requires not the hand of a nobleman to make a lady of her. Heaven has made her one already.

Countess de F. Why, Mr. Hamilton, I should judge you were near the proposing point.

Gab. H. Oh, no, I'm at the other end.

Countess de F. Then you're safe. Look sharp, my dear sir, your countrywomen come here, not to imitate our virtues, but rather to improve on our follies, and I mu t say that the improvement some of them make, speaks well of their abilities.

Gab. H. It's only too true; but then, you know, she's an exception.

Countess de F. It's too bad to have to believe some things, but then, what can one do who has eyes and ears?

Gab. H. To me, she is the spotless one.

Countess de F. Her opinion of you gives your charac-ter considerable color.

Gab. H. True, she has a poor opinion of me, but I know I'm not mistaken in her.

Countess de F. [*Rises and approaches him.*] Gabriel, should I express a worse opinion of you than she, would you exalt me in your heart all the more? If so, hear me. — I call you devil.

Gab. H. Madame, you are a married woman.

Countess de F. A most cruel reminder.

Gab. H. The truth, nevertheless.

Countess de F. Then you scorn my love?

Gab. H. I do not scorn your love, since I respect your husband. 'Tis his, and therefore not yours to give. 'Tis his, although in your keeping, and so beyond my reach to receive, except I play the thief and steal it as I would his purse.

Countess de F. [*Aside.*] Well, there's nothing like desperation to put an end to doubt. [*Laughs merrily.*] Why, sir, such talk as that will make me believe that you think me in earnest. [*Laughs again.*] I see, poor man, that matrimony is the only remedy for your sighs. Well, I presume you'll be satisfied after you get a wife who'll take the sleep out of your eyes, flesh off your bones, money out of your pocket, and put the devil in your heart. As far as being the guardian of a wife's love, I think you'll be like the rest of men, — make a good gallant, but a poor husband. But, pray, Mr. Hamilton, for what did you want to see me?

Gab. H. Madam, as I am about to leave for America, I wish to return you that magnificent present, which I fear you were prompted to send me, under a feeling of obligation for a slight service.I was so fortunate as to render you the first time we met. There, my lady [*Lays a roll of bills on the table*], though I return this to you, 'tis with thanks that are warm with the gratitude of my heart; and madame, I shall ever remember that when you thought me destitute, yours was the hand that sought to help me. [*Enter Earl de F.*]

Earl de F. Ah! A money transaction. Am I to know the secret of the enterprise?

Countess de F. Perhaps Mr. Hamilton will explain.

Gab. H. Certainly. You see, Earl, you're blessed with a charitable wife, who, some time ago, thinking me destitute, sent me this sum of money as a present, which I am about to return to her, — as I'm not in need of it, and about to leave the country.

Earl de F. [*To the Countess.*] Is this the explanation?

Countess de F. I'm sure this is all news to me. I never sent him any money, and he has none to return me. [*Aside.*] I'll teach him what he does, when he flings me back my love. [*Exit Countess de F.*]

Gab. H. [*Aside.*] She don't wish to have *him* know, and so denies it. [*Takes up the bills and puts them in his pocket.*]

Earl de F. Why, sir, did you suppose my wife sent you that money?

Gab. H. Because I knew her to be a friend.

Earl de F. [*With a sneer.*] A friend! But she denies sending it.

Gab. H. Then I'm mistaken.

Earl de F. But, sir, am I mistaken in you?

Gab. H. That depends on what you think of me.

Earl de F. It might not be very flattering to your vanity.

Gab. H. But, perhaps, in keeping with your judgment, — but, sir, as my time is limited, I have the honor of bidding you good day.

Earl de F. Another lover! Oh, hell, give me a thought. [*Re-enter Countess, weeping. Earl, fiercely.*] Well, madame, does it make you weep to think that this new lover is about to leave you?

Countess de F. Oh! I presume 'tis my lot to bear all such now.

Earl de F. Bear what?

Countess de F. . Insult!

Earl de F. You deserve it.

Countess de F. Then you think he was justified in insulting your wife?

Earl de F. Do you refer to this Hamilton? [*She turns away and puts her handkerchief to her eyes.*] So 'twas he; how did he insult you?

Countess de F. As could only a man insult a woman. When I left you with him here, 'twas with an inward struggle to bear up with it for your sake, but since, with it on my mind, I've felt a guilty thing.

Earl de F. Well, I'm glad to find he's not a lover.

Countess de F. [*Throws her arms around his neck.*] Yes, my dear, what you find all the scare-crows of your heart to be.

Earl de F. Ah! There comes Lady Carra; I'll leave you with her. I must see this Hamilton before he quits the hotel. [*Enter Lady Carra, to whom the Earl bows, and then makes his exit.*]

Lady Carra. Why, my dear, what's the matter?

Countess de F. Oh! nothing, only I've been putting the Earl up to fight a duel.

Lady Carra. Then you conspire to be his widow?

Countess de F. I'm sure if a woman ever deserved to be one, I do. Here I've been married a whole year, and my husband alive yet.

Lady Carra. I know how to pity you, my dear, for I was once in a like condition myself.

Countess de F. Oh, well, fortune may smile on me yet.

Lady Carra. And after being a widow three times as I have, then you'll begin to think that the world isn't so bad to you after all.

Countess de F. Ah! my ambition! Shall I ever be a widow three times?

Lady Carra. Why, there's the Countess Tigoris, who has buried three husbands in the creditably short time of three years, and has since been divorced from as many more, and now she's living with her seventh husband, and though they seem to get along pleasantly enough for the present, she vows that she'll never be satisfied till she can count a lord of creation for every finger.

Countess de F. Yes, I remember before I was married how I used to envy her for been able to change her name with every change of season.

Lady Carra. Then, you see, we've both much to live for yet.

Countess de F. Yes, but how she attracts men is more

than I can understand, though I know she's an encouraging example for all homely women who resort to art for their beauty.

Lady Curra.   But what if the Earl should kill Mr. Hamilton, or the reverse should be the case?

Countess de F.   Should the Earl put an end to Mr. Hamilton, then I shall be credited with planting another lover.   If Mr. Hamilton makes a corpse of my dear lord and master, then we shall have a grand funeral and the most appropriate kind of weeds.   I'm sure if the Earl thinks anything of me, he'll be certain to get his quietus, for who should be more willing to gratify the wishes of a wife than a husband.   [*They laugh.*]

Lady Curra.   Indeed, if he don't, in my estimation, it should be held as a sufficient ground for a bill of divorce. But what of the possibility of the Earl's only being wounded?

Countess de F.   Not very encouraging, to be sure, but then, let us hope for the best.   [*Takes her poodle up in her lap and fondles it.*]   Oh! You dear, dear little darling. [*Enter Marquis unseen.*]

Marquis M. M.   Are you speaking to me, my lady?

Countess de F.   Do you suppose I'd talk to a man so, while I've a poodle to pet?

Marquis M. M.   It would be nice, wouldn't it, to be just man enough and poodle enough to please you?

Countess de F.   I find poodles are just splendid to make husbands jealous. I know I never enjoyed married life till I got this one.

Marquis M. M.   [*Pats the dog's head.*]   Yes, he's a nice little fellow.   A pretty little dog.   It's hard to tell which is the better looking, you or your mistress.   But there'd be no doubt about it if you had your ears and tail cut off.

Countess de F.   [*Gets up.*]   Is he a good ratter?   [*To Lady Carra.*]   Come, it seems the Marquis wants more room.

ACT IV.

SCENE I. — *The hotel veranda, music within, dancers can be seen through the windows. Enter Countess de F.*

Countess de F. It's time he was here if he means to meet me. Ah! There he is. [*Exit Countess de F. Enter Earl de F., smoking, walks up and down veranda, then takes chair and sits down. Enter Laura.*]

Laura. Good evening, Earl.

Earl de F. [*Rises.*] Ah! mademoiselle.

Laura. I hope you will excuse me, sir, for again referring to the trouble between you and Mr. Hamilton, but after speaking with you to-day on that subject, I hastened to the Bank de Paris, and there obtained the original order I sent when I directed it to advance him the sum of money which *he* supposed came from your wife. As an American, and a poor student, I then thought him worthy of help. There is the order. [*Gives him a paper.*]

Earl de F. [*Takes the order and reads it by the light of the window.*] It actually proves all you say, — that you sent it and he received it.

Laura. Then, you see, you've proof that he supposed your wife sent it to him.

Earl de F. But, still, nothing to justify his subsequent insults to her.

Laura. Oh! sir, perhaps if all were known, your wife was more mistaken than insulted. I can't bear the thought of being the occasion of this trouble. [*Re-enter Countess de F.*]

Countess de F. Ah! I know I'm intruding, but then, you know, suspicion makes a wife bold.

Earl de F. Suspicion of what?

Countess de F. Nothing, only that you two intend to behave yourselves till you forget.

Earl de F. Madamoiselle, excuse her.

Laura. Certainly. [*Exit Laura.*]

Earl de F. So, madame, you fired your gun.

Countess de F. Yes, my dear, and I hit the mark, too.

Earl de F. Your insinuations were base.

Countess de F. Yes, that is to say, there was some base for my insinuations.

Earl de F. What is it, then?

Countess de F. What does she mean by running around so after you?

Earl de F. Put it as you please. If it is impossible to be on friendly terms with you, 'tis not with the world.

Countess de F. Well, 'tis a relief to see you taking up with other company than mine, and I truly trust, sir, that there'll be no betrayal of confidence on your part. [*Exit Countess de F.*]

Earl de F. Jealous! And really for the first time to my knowledge. Indeed, and so I must be of some consequence, after all, but soon she'll find how she wrongs me. Yes, I will despatch the challenge to him at once. [*Exit the Earl. Re-enter Gabriel and Countess de F. Countess looks cautiously around.*]

Countess de F. They all seem to be engaged in the dance. But as I was going to remark, it is not on my account that he seeks to revenge himself on you.

Gab. H. Then pray what does he mean by declaring that I insulted you?

Countess de F. That's but a mere pretence, while the real cause is his infatuation for Miss Laura. [*Gabriel turns away.*] There, and you doubt it, though you saw them meeting clandestinely here, and exchanging letters, but a moment ago. This is not the first time either that I've parted them. If it were, she might be excused, but as they meet as often as the occasion will permit, why, with me, as his wife, it is becoming a serious matter.

Gab. H. Then you think she's infatuated with him.

Countess de F. He seems encouraged.

Gab. H. It's not credible.

Countess de F. You forget, that in her eyes he is a nobleman.

Gab. H. It can't be that she's so foolish and heartless.

Countess de F. If she were not heartless, after having saved her life, as you did, she would have made you the god of the heaven of her love. [*Re-enter Laura B.,*

*meeting them face to face.   Exit Gabriel and Countess
de F.*]

Laura.   So this is the man on whom my love doats,
dreams, and lives.   [*Looks around.*]   I thought I'd still
find the Earl here, and get that order back again.   [*Enter
Marquis Max Muddle.*]

Marquis M. M.   Ah! Miss Laura, I thought you were
out here, for I could not see a star, and so concluded you
were on the eclipsing business.

Laura.   Sir!

Marquis M. M.   Miss Laura, I've been wanting to
propose to you for a long time.   [*She turns away.*]   Oh,
Laura, if you only knew what was in my throat, you'd
pity me.   Yes, the sweet lullaby of my heart is your own
pet name.   Fair angel, you never loved yourself better than
I love you.   [*Enter Mrs. B.   The Marquis holds down his
head.*]   [*Aside.*]   Let me see, what was I about to say
next.   [*Aloud.*]   You see, they all say that I'm in love.   I
don't know, but suppose they know best; and my friends
at the club say that 'tis high time I had a wife under con-
trol, and was tuning up the discords of married life.   My
mother says of course I love you, as you have a great fortune, and I a great many wants, and so I've concluded to
make the best of you.   I'm a Marquis,— I suppose you
know what that means, if not, by and by, when I won't
be bothered courting you, I'll tell you all about it.   And,
come to think of it, I'm a man of many superior points.
Not a porcupine, but a good enough kind for a woman's
superior, provided she don't try the henpecking business.
[*Mrs. M. approaches.*]   But one thing I want understood before you take advantage of me.   [*Laura turns
away and walks off.*]   I don't want any rheumatic,
hysterical females around me; not that I object to
your grandmother's having the rheumatism or hysterics,
and taking them to bed with her, but I *do* object to
being put in the same bed.   No; I don't want any such
a female around me, always sporting a wrinkle on her
nose.   You see my eccentricities are of a peculiar type,
with strong odor of contempt for females of the mother-
in-law persuasion.   Besides, you know, when a man has a
wife, she's enough for him to contend with, without having

her grandmother around with her, always destroying hap
piness and mixing the devil up with politeness. [*Looks
up and finds that instead of talking to Laura, he has been
addressing Mrs. B. Falls backwards over the veranda,
and holds on with his hands and feet.*]

Mrs. B. It's too bad you're not hanging by the neck.
[*Exit Mrs. B.*]

Marquis M. M. Oh! dear, I've fainted. Give me
air, brandy. Am I drunk, or only intoxicated? [*Lets
himself down on the lawn, then gets up and rubs
himself.*] Talk about astronomical discoveries, and
stars; — why here's a whole system just come to light;
that was quite a fall for a little ways. I wonder if any
one took me for a falling star or an asteroid. But I had
supposed that that antiquarian apparition had shuffled
her coil by this time, given the old man the variations of
bedtime in a high key, and now had her snoring abilities
well tuned. Perhaps she'll only take what I said for an
honest opinion, or possibly think that my eccentricities
were merely on a spree. [*Re-enter Gab. H. and Countess
de F.*]

Countess de F. No, not that I really sent the money,
but knew of it. Oh, no, I wasn't to be caught in such a
scrape, but if I didn't send it, a friend did. So, before
I'm missed, — good-night. Angels in thy dreams, and
may the fates preserve thee till we meet again. [*Throws
him a kiss. They exit in different directions.*]

Marquis M. M. Yum, yum. It's all hug and hug with
them. She don't seem to be very particular whether she
make a devil or an angel out of the Earl, provided she
only has the pleasure of crying at his funeral.

SCENE II. — *Drawing-room. Discovered Laura and the
Marquis.*

Laura. I shall never forget that I owe my life to Mr.
Hamilton.

Marquis M. M. Nor can I forget that I think just as
much of you, as though I had saved your life myself.
Indeed, I couldn't improve on your feelings if I were your
husband.

Laura. Oh! Then it didn't lower me in your estimation at all to have been saved by Mr. Hamilton?

Marquis M. M. Not in the least. Do you think
such a small thing as that would make me change my
mind?

Laura. I don't know ; you men are so fickle.

Marquis M. M. That's a contagion that never
attacked me.

Laura. It may be hereditary.

Marquis M. M. But I'm not one of the tubercular
tribe. Besides, I know my place as a live beau, if I'm
only encouraged.

Laura. There, Marquis, do tell me some of your good
points. Why, one would think you were a pirate to hear
you talk so about yourself.

Marquis M. M. Well, I love dogs ; — a good habit,
isn't it? I also practice my affections on horses, just to
keep them in working order, you know, till I get married.
Then I indulge my ardor in champagne, which shows
consistency in full bloom ; and cards, though a tricky
amusement, have the elements of innocence and old maids
in them. Then my other accomplishments will bear
special notice after I get married.

Laura. [*Sorrowfully.*] Is that all?

Marquis M. M. Oh, no ; you see with my love
divided between my wife and such accomplishments, that
she'll really get the better of me. And above all, I'll be
her right-hand man, and she will find me worth being jealous
of, too, if I know myself. I'm no fool, as you can see,
if you've taken the trouble to observe. Perhaps you've
already noticed it.

Laura. So you think that if some lady would be
satisfied with any kind of a husband, you'd make a very
good one.

Marquis M. M. Not exactly, though that's a point in
my favor ; but if she'd only be contented with a good combination of matrimonial points, she'd find I'd do without
much courting.

Laura. Then you don't think much of courting?

Marquis M. M. Not to speak of. You see this
swapping sighs and smiles for a half dozen years, is a
loss of time, and time's money, and money makes the
mare go. Besides, they never really know each other

till after they've harvested some matrimonial bliss. But, by the way, courting does well enough if there's an occasional marriage mixed in with it now and then. You see it takes the curse off ; don't you think so?

Laura.   Then after all, you really believe in marriage.

Marquis M. M.   Oh, yes, as it makes squabbling legal and binding. So my idea is, that if after a longer or shorter observation of what we can see, we mutually agree or coincide that we're fitted to make mates in the same hymeneal nest ; why it's a mere waste of ammunition to further continue negotiations.

Laura.   Then you don't think much of a courting skirmish?

Marquis M. M.   No, give me the pitched battle ; the sooner the agony, the shorter the dread.

Laura.   Indeed! Yours is a religious submission.

Marquis M. M.   Rather acquiescing to the inevitable ; however, I believe in making marriage nip courting in the bud, and so stop all superfluous talk about the matter.

Laura.   But suppose a young lady wishes to find out something of her lover's character, why, you see, courting gives her an opportunity.

Marquis M. M.   Oh! She'd find him out soon enough after marriage, I can assure you. Besides, if he's an honest fellow, he'd tell her all about it. Why, I never gave any woman a chance to blackmail me, nor did I ever lay myself liable to a breach of promise.   I never broke anybody's heart, that I know of. My morals are all intact and in good working order. Morally, I never committed suicide ; in fact, I never committed myself in any way ; so to pop the issue, if you've been sent into the world to be my wife, I don't object. In fact, I'm willing to put up with my fate. Now if you'll accept my hand, heart, fortune, and name, I'm yours. I know I've asked you this question before, and, getting no answer, I took your silence for consent.   But I thought I'd ask you now to confirm it.

Laura.   Why, Marquis, you're very kind.

Marquis M. M.   Don't mention it.

Laura.   But you overpower me so.

Marquis M. M.   Well, I always like to do the good thing.

Laura. But come to think of it, I shall have to give you up.

Marquis M. M. [*Drops on his knees, hurting them. Aside.*] Oh, my knees! [*Rubs his knees.*] This, dear Laura, is only a part of what I have suffered for you. [*Rubs his knees again.*] Would you leave me a prey to the fury of my nature?

Laura. [*Takes up a book and commences to read. Yawning.*] I must refer you to my grandparents.

Marquis M. M. Your parents never loved you as I do. I could swim the ocean for you.

Laura. And really, can you swim?

Marquis M. M. Yes; and I could go through fire for you.

Laura. Well now, come to think of it, you have proved yourself a good salamander. [*Enter Mrs. B. followed by Mr. B.*] I think you had better see my grandmother.

Marquis M. M. Oh! Laura, let us take each other into consideration, and grandmothers be ignored.

Mrs. B. Laura, what is the meaning of this?

Laura. Oh! nothing very serious.

Marquis M. M. No, madame, I only wish your daughter well, and so would wed her.

Mrs. B. Sir, for you to look me in the face is insult.

Marquis M. M. My dear madame, I was only fooling the other night.

Mrs. B. And then you made quite a successful fool.

Marquis M. M. [*Gets up.*] Madame, you're a woman.

Mrs. B. I can't call you a man.

Marquis M. M. Madame, I shall have the honor of bidding you an eternal farewell.

Mrs. B. Thank you. [*Marquis starts to go.*]

Mr. B. Sir, have you been insulting these ladies?

Marquis M. M. Do you insinuate?

Mr. B. No, sir, I mean it.

Marquis M. M. Then I don't take it.

Mr. B. All right; but I was thinking if you did, how nicely 'twould fit you.

Marquis M. M. I don't understand.

Mr. B.   Oh! I only mean that I haven't fought a duel since I've been in France, but hope soon to have an opportunity.

Marquis M. M.   A cause for one may gratify you.

Mr. B.   Sir, you're a scoundrel.

Marquis M. M.   You're wrongly informed.

Mr. B.   You lie, like a town clock. [*Exit Marquis in a hurry. Mr. B. takes off his collar.*] There, my dear, I've ruptured a button. I think you had better repair it at once. [*Exit Mr. and Mrs. B. Enter Gabriel. Laura rises.*]

Gab. H.   Miss Bliss, on returning late to my apartments last night, I found your order awaiting me, and so concluded 'twould be well to refund you the money at once. [*Takes out paper and roll of bills and lays them on the table.*] There, I think you'll find here the whole amount I received, with interest.

Laura.   [*Aside.*]   I might have known she would get that order from the Earl, and give it to him.

Gab. H.   I supposed, madame, you looked for this visit, or I would not have made myself a subject of annoyance to you.

Laura.   [*Aside.*]   The idea—just as if I had sent it to him as a hint for him to return the money.   [*To G.*]   I can assure you this visit was unexpected.

Gab. H.   True, I might have sent the money to you by another person, or have placed it in the bank at your disposal, but then I thought your kindness in that act, worthy of my personal thanks.

Laura.   [*Aside.*]   He comes late with his thanks, knowing all along that I sent it.

Gab. H.   To learn to-day that you were the author of this kindness, makes it vain for my lips to attempt my heart's bidding. [*She turns away from him and sits down. He bows and retires.*]

Laura.   Gabriel, Mr. Hamilton, please be seated. [*She looks up and starts to find him gone.*] What, have I driven him from me? Not even asked him to be seated! 'Twas an insult. How modest, gentlemanly, and yet that woman's lover? And for the full love of my heart, nothing to offer me but such. No, my woman's pride must bear me up, and let him go his way. [*Enter Earl de F.*]

Earl de F. Mademoiselle, I fear I have made a grievous mistake, an unpardonable blunder.

Laura. Indeed !

Earl de F. Yes, by losing the order you gave me last night.

Laura. [*Takes up order and money from the table.*] I see you did, and here it is, having but just been returned to me.

Earl de F. By whom?

Laura. The last person in the world whom I would have know that it was I who sent it.

Earl de F. But how came he by it?

Laura. Ask the Countess ; no doubt she could inform you.

Earl de F. You wrong her. She never saw it, much less gave it to any one. [*Enter Countess de F.*]

Countess de F. You see, my dear, I shall be on hand when you attempt to elope.

Earl de F. 'Twill be very kind of you to see me off.

Countess de F. Yes, and a great pleasure ; ahem !

Earl de F. Madame, we've been discussing a lost paper, and the probability of your having found it.

Countess de F. [*Takes a letter out of her pocket and holds it up in his face.*] Is that it?

Earl de F. [*Takes letter and reads it.*] Fury ! This is the challenge that I sent to that Hamilton.

Countess de F. Did you expect him to find it in my desk ?

Earl de F. [*Aside.*] This is what I left there last night instead of the affectionate letter that I wrote her saying I would defend her honor in the morning, if need be with my life?

Countess de F. Sir, what is the meaning of this?

Earl de F. Good heavens ! I'll be made a butt of ridicule from one end of the continent to the other.

Countess de F. To be sure.

Earl de F. Here I've already posted him a coward in public print, for not meeting me, though I never challenged him,— challenged my wife !

Countess de F.   Yes, and if you don't make a suitable apology, I may see fit to accept.

Earl de F.   Oh, fool, fool that I am.

Countess de F.   [*Aside.*]   That's what I always told him, but he's only just beginning to understand himself.

Earl de F.   [*To Laura.*]   Then 'twas Mr. Hamilton himself who returned that order to you?

Laura.   It was, sir.

Earl de F.   Yes, and I sent it to him last night instead of a challenge, which was intended ; — enclosed the challenge to my wife in place of a letter, and made a fool of myself all round.   [*Enter Marquis M. M., reading a paper.*]

Marquis M. M.   I say, Earl, here it is.   [*Holds the paper up to him.*]   See.   [*Points and reads.*]   " I hereby brand Gabriel Hamilton a coward." Signed. Earl de Foy.

Earl de F.   Take it away ; the thought of it is enough.

Marquis M. M.   Why, Earl, this is an accusation to be proud of.   [*Re-enter Gabriel with Mrs. B. on his arm, followed by Mr. B.*]

Mrs. B.   You see, Laura will want to thank you, too, when she hears that it was you who saved my life as well as her own.

Laura.   [*Coolly.*]   So, grandma, you've found your hero.

Mrs. B.   Yes, and indeed, Mr. Hamilton, I think you were very selfish.   Here you've gone, as I might say, and saved the lives of a whole family, and then walked off without giving us even a chance to thank you.   I really believe that if it were not for the gendarme who assisted you on the ladder the night of the fire, and who since promised to find out who you were, as he did just now, when he pointed you out to me in the office, I should still be in ignorance of who my preserver was.

Gab. H.   Virtue, madame, is its own reward.

Laura.   I fear, grandma, we shall be in his debt forever.

Gab. H.   To see you both alive and well, cancels all obligations.

Marquis M. M.   That reminds me of what Countess

de Foy said to you on the veranda the other dark night. [*Stops a moment.*] Ah! I have it, — "May the fates preserve thee till some other dark night."

Mrs. B. On the veranda last night with the Countess! Not the last person in the world to make such a mistake.

Earl de F. Be careful how you make such statements.

Marquis M. M. That's as much as to say the worst inclinations of my tongue have been having fair play.

Earl de F. I'm glad you understand me.

Marquis M. M. Sir, this is a direct denial that you insinuate.

Earl de F. Take it as best suits your temper.

Marquis M. M. Be careful, Earl; of late you've been lucky in challenging a coward, but perhaps fortune might fail you in a second attempt.

Gab. H. Yes, my humble opinion is, that the man who cares to fight the Marquis, is ripe for eternity.

Laura. In the interest of peace, I've this to say, the Marquis' statement is true.

Earl de F. True?

Mrs. B. [*To Laura.*] Do you know what you say?

Laura. I saw them there, myself, at the time mentioned.

Countess de F. Oh, to be sure, but if you hadn't been there indulging in little secrecies with a married man, you and he wouldn't be so shocked at the idea of Mr. Hamilton and myself meeting there and speaking.

Mrs. B. [*To Laura.*] You on the veranda at night with the Earl, indulging in secrecies!

Laura. I did speak to him there last evening on a ·matter of business.

Countess de F. Yes, some folks do transact business in the dark.

Earl de F. About that matter, I have this to say : — Last evening, Miss Bliss, here, in the interests of peace, and to prevent bloodshed, if possible, between Mr. Hamilton and me, gave me a paper which he had obtained late during the day, [*to Gabriel*] which paper, you, sir, received from me last night by mistake, instead of a challenge.

Mrs. B.   But why a challenge?

Earl de F.   For insult to the Countess.

Gab. H.   She claims no insult, but rather that you, infatuated with Miss Laura, seek to meet me as a rival.

Countess de F.   [*Aside.*]   Beat at my own game!

Earl de F.   Goddess of iniquity, what does this mean?

Countess de F.   [*Indignantly.*]   That you meet your man, but in the wrong field, and with harmless weapons.   [*Gab. H. takes a letter out of his pocket.   Aside.*]   Dare he betray me for those unguarded words I've just uttered?

Gab. H.   Hitherto I considered your wife a friend of mine, but recent events prove that I have been mistaken.

Earl de F.   But what reason had you for thinking she sent you that sum of money?

Gab. H.   She professed to be my friend, when friends with me were scarce in Paris; then she even tacitly admitted sending me that money; thus was I led to look upon her as a friend, whose goodness sought to help me as a needy person.   There, sir, is a note that I but recently received from her, and I think you will find that it explains itself.

Countess de F.   Coward!   You're not worthy of my contempt.

Earl de F.   [*Reads the note aloud.*]   "To Mr. Hamilton: *My dear Friend, — I fear you misunderstood me about that money affair.   If so, please meet me on the veranda this evening, and I will explain.   Be sure and come, and you will find mine the friendship that you can swear by.   Your faithful friend, Countess de Foy.*"   [*To the Countess.*]   Woman!   What, he your dear friend after insulting you?   Yours the friendship for him to swear by, though having basely insulted you?   You his faithful friend, though he at deadly enmity with your husband?

Countess de F.   It only means that when you make a carcass of that man's body, you will have a wife's respect and thanks.   Coward, I but urged on your prey, thinking that, as a man, you would make sport of his life.   It's too bad, my dear, you were so unfortunate as to make such a blunder; just think of it, had you met, perhaps you would both be in heaven now.   I always did think you'd make a better angel than a husband, and he a more profound cherub than a man. But don't let me interrupt you ; go on, dally, dally with the ex-valet ; you'll find him willing, no doubt, to hob-nob with a poltroon. Afterwards, my love, come to me, and perhaps it may be convenient to proceed to solemnize our divorce. [*Exit Countess, with a sweep.*]

Earl de F. I find, sir, that under the circumstances, I have deeply wronged you.

Gab. H. And been sorely wronged yourself.

Earl de F. Ah, but I would to God it were you who had wronged me and not she ; but as it is, to insist on your meeting me at the mere instigation of her whim, would be to still acknowledge myself her slave, which I will never do again, while there's freedom in a separation ; so in all justice to you and myself for posting you a coward, I will publicly retract. [*Bows and exits.*]

Lady M. M. Marquis, I want your arm. [*The Marquis gives her his arm and they move toward the door, as if to go.*] My errand here to-day, madame, was to insist on withdrawing my proposition in behalf of the Marquis for the hand of your granddaughter. Recent events demand that I take this course in order to defend his honor and good name.

Mrs. B. You've nothing to withdraw ; the Marquis got his answer to-day, on his knees, after which he bade us an eternal farewell, which I shall be pleased to see take place.

Lady M. M. So, fool, you've been on your knees again?

Marquis M. M. They deserve to be blackmailed.

Lady M. M. Blockhead! [*Exit Marquis and Lady M. M.*]

Mr. B. Well, my dear, how is your taste for blood, now?

Mrs. B. All gone.

Mr. B. Good, 'twas poor taste.

Mrs. B. And one on which, I trust, we'll never again differ.

Mr. B. Then we are to agree that blood's but blood, and men but men.

Laura. So, grandma, Mr. Hamilton really saved your life, too.

Mrs. B. Yes, Laura, and very ungrateful have we been to him.

Laura. Then let him name his reward, and if not too late, perhaps we can make him amends.

Gab. H. I've not forgotten your golden thanks.

Laura. [*Aside.*] How stupid men are! [*To Gab. H.*] Mr. Hamilton, I see all, now, and though I wronged you, 'twas an honest mistake, and now that we really know you, I can truly say, it is with regret I see you about to leave us. [*Gab. H. looks at her in amazement.*]

Gab. H. Well, this pays me for all wrongs and mistakes.

Laura. You seem easily satisfied.

Gab. H. The beggar must be satisfied with what he gets, besides, even this from you is more than I expected.

Laura. Ah, but if the beggar takes a mere pittance when the board is spread before him, what would you say?

Gab. H. [*Looks doubtfully at her.*] I should say, why, — that he wasn't very hungry.

Laura. [*Aside.*] Dear me, how stupid! I'll just kiss him if I get a good chance. [*To Gabriel.*] Mr. Hamilton, will you even allow us to pay interest on the debt we owe you? [*Approaches him.*]

Gab. H. Madame, you owe me nothing.

Laura. [*Aside.*] Oh, dear, I don't know but I shall have to get grandpa and ma to hold him for me.

Gab. H. Is it possible that she wishes to taunt me?

Laura. Then my life in your eyes is a mere nothing!

Gab. H. Laura, I beg pardon, Miss ——

Laura. Please don't be particular about calling me Miss; but perhaps you don't care to call me Laura, now.

Gab. H. [*Advances towards her and takes her hands.*] No, not Laura, unless 'tis Laura, my little wife.

Laura. What am I to expect in the future, if you begin to call me names already?

Gab. H. But how is it, is this the sacrifice of your heart and hand?

Laura. Now knowing you never to have been the

Countess's lover, I make my choice among the world's millions. [*He kisses her; Mrs. B. approaches them.*] What say you, grandma, shall our preserver be thus rewarded? [*Kisses him.*]

Mrs. B. Yes, my child, you owe him a life's devotion. What say you, father, do you consent?

Mr. B. I have to say that she, like her grandmother, has an eye for a good-looking man, and one as good as he is good-looking, eh, my dear? Yes, they have my consent if their hearts are in the matter. [*Enter Madame and Mabel Buzot.*]

Mad. B. We thought, Mr. Hamilton, we'd step in a moment to see you, as we just heard that you are about to return to America, but should judge by appearances that congratulations were more in order than adieux.

Gab. H. It was my intention to leave for America at once, but I've changed my mind, and concluded to postpone the trip for the present. As for congratulations, madame, I'm happy to say that they are in order.

Mad. B. Then I presume your friends here, now understand that you're not the poor, virtuous young man that they at first took you to be, but rather the profligate of a large fortune, who has been amusing himself at theirs and other folks' expense?

Gab. H. I must confess that I have misled them as to the extent of my fortune, but doubt your ability, madame, to deceive them with regard to my real character.

Mab. B. Then we'll leave it for you to do. [*Exit Madame and Mabel B.*]

Gab. H. Laura, as some one had the goodness the first time we met, to report me to be nobody but a poor student, for your sake I let the story go uncontradicted.

Laura. For my sake?

Gab. H. Yes, you were then reported to be in search of a title to wed; this, my love for you would not let me believe, and so I put it to the test, and found that it was right. [*Puts his arm around her.*] Eh? [*She lays her head upon his shoulder. Re-enters Marquis with a revolver in each hand.*]

Marquis M. M.　I am not ashamed to say, Miss Laura, that I'm about to die.　Yes, I've come to make good my eternal farewell as becomes the man who loves you, — that is, if you haven't thought me worth a second consideration.

Gab. H.　Look here, Marquis, I thought you came here to kill yourself.

Marquis M. M.　I did, but don't you be in too big a hurry.

Gab. H.　But you know time is money.

Mr. B.　By the way, Marquis, if there's any way that we can assist you in this matter, we shall be very happy to do so.

Marquis M. M.　Thank you, but this isn't much of a job ; I've done it before.

Gab. H.　Now Marquis, if you mean business, just stick the muzzle of a revolver in each ear and I'll give you the word.　[*The Marquis points a revolver towards each ear.*]　Now then.

Marquis M. M.　What, now?

Gab. H.　No, not now, but after I count three.　Now, one, two—.　[*The Marquis fires both revolvers over his head.*]　I should judge, Marquis, that you never had much practice in committing suicide.

Marquis M. M.　Well, to be candid, I haven't indulged in a matter of this kind lately.

Gab. H.　Now then, suppose you try it again ; this time you may succeed in getting the whole top of your head off.

Marquis M. M.　The whole top of my head off—why that'd spoil my hair.

Gab. H.　Never mind, we'll see that it's oiled and combed all right again.

Marquis M. M.　[*Points the revolvers at his head, and takes them down again.*]　Don't forget that I part my hair on the left side.

Mr. B.　Certainly, and we'll see that your jaw is tied up, and your eyes closed ; and, by the way, I presume you'd like to be put on ice, at once?

Marquis M. M.　What, and freeze me to death?

Gab. H.　Suppose you put the muzzles of your revolvers in your mouth this time. [*The Marquis puts the muzzles of his revolvers in his mouth.*] Now then.

Marquis M. M. What, now?

Gab. H. No, when I give the word,—now, one, two—

Marquis M. M. [*Takes the revolvers out of his mouth.*] Confound them, they won't go off. [*Examines them and they go off as if by accident.*]

Gab. H. Let me see one of them. [*Takes one of the revolvers.*] There, while I'm examining this one, you can try the other one again. [*Gab. H. fires it out of the window.*]

Marquis M. M. This is a very nice carpet, isn't it.

Mr. B. Yes, 'tis a fine article to fall on.

Marquis M. M. Wouldn't it be too bad to spoil it with my blood?

Mr. B. Well, I admit it'd make it a second-hand affair, but then it deserves a pretty good article.

Gab. H. Go on, Marquis, if you spoil it, we'll take up a subscription and replace it. [*Fires the other revolver out of the window.*] Why, this is all right; you ought to be able to kill yourself every time with it.

Mr. B. Yes, Marquis, and as far as we are concerned you shall have all the respect due a corpse.

Gab. H. So you see there isn't the slightest reason in the world why you shouldn't blow your head off.

Marquis M. M. If I could only be persuaded.

Gab. H. [*Gives him the revolver.*] Be careful, that's your last shot.

Marquis M. M. Is it? [*Fires it off as if by accident.*] Just my luck. [*Re-enter Lady M. M., with a scream, followed by Lady Carra, Countess de Foy, Madame and Mabel B., Lord Carra and Earl de Foy. Marquis M. M. points both revolvers at the ladies, they scream.*] Stand back; I'm in no mood to be trifled with now; I am about to take a lover's leap into eternity, and if you wish to be calm spectators of how the thing is done, why, I've no objections; but if any one of you goes to kicking up a rumpus or a bluster, by all the furies of desperation, I'll not take this leap alone. [*He points the revolvers at his head, and with a scream, Lady M. M. springs forward and grasps one of his arms, followed by Lady Carra, who grasps the other one.*]

Marquis M. M.   There's no use in trying to die; everything's against me.

CURTAIN.

An Original Comedy,

IN FOUR ACTS.

By JOHN J. FOX, M. D.

BOSTON:
PRINTED BY J. W. PITMAN & SON,
No. 23 WATER STREET.
1879.